# HIS
# DOUBLE
# LIFE

## BOOKS BY NICOLE TROPE

# HIS
# DOUBLE
# LIFE

## NICOLE TROPE

*bookouture*

Published by Bookouture in 2024

An imprint of Storyfire Ltd.
Carmelite House
50 Victoria Embankment
London EC4Y 0DZ

www.bookouture.com

ISBN: 978-1-83525-108-9
eBook ISBN: 978-1-83525-107-2

*For Jacob*
*Over to you now.*
*Don't worry – I'll figure out the TV*

# PROLOGUE

When Rowan comes bolting into the kitchen first, Diana doesn't think to worry.

'I win, I win,' her ten-year-old son shouts, jumping up and down, his cheeks red with exhilaration and triumph.

'Well done,' she says, smiling. 'Where's the soccer ball?'

'Sawyer is carrying it,' puffs Rowan. 'Dad, can you take us for donuts? Sawyer wants one too,' he says to his father.

Leo looks up from his phone, his attention dragged back into the kitchen and the interruption of the peaceful Sunday morning.

'Yeah, maybe, I need to do some work first,' he says, standing and leaving the room, his study door immediately slamming deliberately shut.

Diana watches her son's face fall. 'I'll take you, as soon as Sawyer gets back,' she says.

'Okay,' says Rowan but he is still disappointed. It's not the treat he craves but time with his father.

Diana stands and begins cleaning up the remains of the breakfast dishes while Rowan slumps in a chair to wait for his twin brother.

'Why is he taking so long? He's so slooow,' whines Rowan.

Diana feels a tickle of alarm. Why *is* he taking so long? Each Sunday morning since they have been allowed to walk to the park alone, the boys have raced each other back. Rowan always wins but Sawyer is never very far behind. The park is one block away and they don't even have to cross a road to get there. It's part of the reason why she was so delighted with the location of this house. It's far enough away to allow a modicum of independence for the boys since they celebrated their tenth birthdays, but still close enough so Diana doesn't worry about them in their safe neighbourhood.

'Go and check where he is,' says Diana, and Rowan obediently jumps off the chair and darts out of the kitchen door to the back garden and the gate that leads to the road behind the house. He will be able to see his brother coming just by stepping out onto the pavement.

After a moment, Diana follows him. Sawyer may have decided against a race today. It's not easy to always come second. Perhaps he decided he didn't even feel like the competition.

The street behind the house is empty of people and filled with morning birdsong from the lorikeets and the distant sound of traffic on the highway. The air holds the wintry chill of an August day.

Sawyer is nowhere in sight.

The tickle of alarm grows more urgent. 'Can you run back to the park and see where he is, please?' says Diana, but as Rowan starts to move, she grabs him, instinct telling her he should not go alone. 'No, wait, I'll come with you, just let me tell Dad and get some shoes.'

She turns to go back inside when her phone vibrates in her pocket. Pulling it out automatically, she sees a text on the screen.

*If you want Sawyer to come home, your husband needs to tell the truth.*

'Come on, Mum,' says Rowan. Diana is frozen, staring at the screen. The morning sounds disappear. She no longer feels the cold.

'Mum, come on,' says Rowan again.

Everything springs into sharp focus, her feet in thick black socks, the rumble of a truck far away, the smell of smoke from a chimney. 'No,' she shouts, 'no, go back in the house,' utter terror making her voice shrill.

'But I want to go for donuts. I'll be really fast.'

'Back in the house,' she yells again and then she grabs him and pulls him inside the garden, closing the gate behind her. What on earth is going on? Her heart races, anxiety and fear making her feel sick. How on earth can this be happening?

'Get in the house, Rowan,' she commands and her son complies, unused to her raising her voice. 'And go upstairs, just go upstairs, okay.'

'Okay,' he says and she doesn't look at him because she knows she will see confusion there and she cannot explain anything now.

Opening the study door, she startles her husband who is on his computer, his fingers moving over the keys.

'I'm—' he begins to say.

'Leo,' she gasps, shoving the phone right up to his face, showing him the text. 'What have you done? What does this mean? Who is this from?'

He looks at the screen, incomprehension on his face for only a moment before he groans. 'No, no, oh God, no.'

'What have you done, Leo?' Diana repeats, tears filling her eyes. 'What have you done?'

# PART ONE

# ONE

## SERENA

Five Weeks Ago

Swiping the lipstick across her lips in one smooth motion, she watches the rapid change of colour from light pink to a deep, dark red. The lipstick was expensive and not a colour she ever wears but the name, VIXEN, printed in small black letters at the bottom of the tube, felt like a sign. After blotting her lips with a tissue, she smiles at herself in the mirror. 'Hello,' she whispers, dropping her tone.

Turning to check the back of her outfit, she admires the way the blue fitted dress dips low at the back, showing off her smooth skin. Also expensive, also not what she would usually wear.

Blue is a good colour for her olive skin tone and it brings out the blue in her eyes as well. She turns back to the mirror, lifting her silky-smooth black hair and then letting it drop again. She usually wears her hair up, but he will like it hanging long against her back. He looks like the type of man who would.

The low hum of three hundred real-estate agents all discussing just how well they're doing can be heard even in this hotel bathroom where the walls are thick with cream marble tiles.

Out in the conference room, perfume and heavy cologne mingle, creating a soup of artificial scent. The salty smell of the ocean, only metres away, is locked out of the hotel by the stale air conditioning. Winter has arrived everywhere in Australia but Queensland, where the state seems reluctant to let go of summer, even now at the end of June. Serena likes the warmth in the air, hates being inside, but what she likes and doesn't like is not important right now.

She's planned how she will do this, played out the scene in her mind again and again. But now that she's here, her mouth is dry and her heart racing. *This is wrong, so wrong. This is another woman's husband. This is someone's life.*

Smoothing the dress over her hips, she silences the voice. She's doing what needs to be done. And he has a choice. He will very definitely have a choice. In an hour she could walk out of here and get back on a plane and return to Sydney and this whole trip would have been wasted but she's pretty sure that won't happen. Pretty sure but not completely sure.

Another woman walks into the bathroom and Serena catches the envious glance. She's ready. He won't be able to resist her.

'I'm Serena Burns, commercial real estate. I'm Serena Burns, commercial real estate.' She smiles as the phrase circles in her head. She likes the surname Burns. Likes that she sees a glowing yellow-orange flame every time she thinks about it. *Burns. It burns. I will burn.*

She's not in real estate, certainly not in commercial real estate.

But then, she's not Serena Burns either.

# TWO

## LEO

Five Weeks Ago

He drains the second whisky faster than he should have but screw it – it's all free and the whisky is cheap, thin and light, tasting of nothing much. Next to him, Jason Black is going on and on about his latest twenty-million-dollar house sale and Leo would like to grab the dapper little man by his throat and slowly squeeze the words out of him.

'And while I can't tell you exactly who bought the house, all you need to do is think about a movie that only came out a few months ago and has already made millions at the box office and you'll know just who it is.' He laughs and Leo watches the others standing in the group immediately look down at their phones, googling to find the famous, mysterious new owner of the waterfront property. Jason Black meets Leo's gaze and offers him a generous-toothed smile.

Leo struggles to return the smile, settling for a nod. Leo knows he should be the one earning the commission on multi-million-dollar deals, not this little gnome of a man with his pointed bright-blue shoes. *Who wears a colour like that?*

'I may just get another one,' says Leo, as Jason begins a new story about overseas buyers with wads of cash to spend who wanted to fly him out to their private islands for a chat.

Jason raises his eyebrows at Leo's rudeness, nodding. 'Sure, Leo, sure. We'll catch up again.' Jason is a year younger than Leo and they both started in real estate, managing rentals and learning on the job, at the same time.

Leo turns away, not offering to bring Jason a drink. The man is insufferable but everyone loves him. He's charming and brings gifts and talks fast and he gets results, his reputation feeding off itself as buyers and sellers alike seek him out. He turns over the biggest properties in Sydney with ease and each huge sale leads to another huge sale. Leo hates him with a passion.

He moves across the conference room where you can almost smell the envy in the air as small-time agents listen to those who have conquered the property market expound their theories for great sales. 'It's luck and timing,' Leo would like to shout. This year his timing is off and his luck seems to be on vacation.

He pulls at his striped tie and moves his shoulders in his expensive suit, smiling and nodding at men and women he knows, admiring a shapely form now and again. Last year he managed a quick hook-up with a woman from Melbourne, Rachel or Riley, something like that. She was only twenty-three and so gorgeous it made Leo want to cry as he ran his hands over her smooth pale skin and breathed in her soap-fresh scent.

The first time he slept with someone at a conference was four years ago and guilt had gnawed at him for days. The second time, which happened the following year, was easier but he still felt guilty when he got home.

But within days he began to anticipate the next conference and the next time he could just let go of his mundane existence.

He has a nice life, what anyone would think is a nice life – wife, twin ten-year-old boys and a house in the suburbs, a safe neighbourhood, with a pool out the back, expensive car and a good wine collection. And an overwhelming desire to ask, 'Is that all there is?'

As he gets in line for the bar set up on one side of the hall, he thinks about Diana who will be getting ready to pick up the kids from school around now.

At breakfast yesterday, before he left for the conference in the Queensland sunshine, he had taken a moment to study her as she slumped in the chair at the whitewashed kitchen table. Her dressing gown was an unattractive pink lumpy material that completely covered her body. She rarely puts on make-up these days except when they're out with friends but when she does, she still resembles the woman he met fifteen years ago.

She had been sitting two seats away in the crowded bar, nursing a cocktail and looking around as the two young women next to her, obviously her friends, had chatted and laughed. Leo had been trying to order another beer, waving his hands to get the bartender's attention when they'd locked eyes. Diana had smiled at his exaggerated gestures. And Leo had been unable to stop himself from smiling back. She was dressed in tight blue jeans and a lace crop top and her brown eyes had sparkled with an invitation he couldn't refuse.

Then, he had been twenty-eight, the same age as she was, and he'd felt like the world was his oyster. The night they'd met he had just sold an apartment with harbour views from one window for over a million dollars. That's small change now for such an apartment these days but, at the time, it had felt like an enormous sum. Leo had been able to see his whole brilliant career laid out before him.

'Can I buy you a drink?' he'd asked, moving towards her and giving up on getting the bartender's attention until he was standing next to a good-looking woman.

'I don't know, can you?' she'd giggled, and he'd laughed along with her. She had been enchanting back then.

They used to have a lot to say to each other but somewhere between the twins arriving and now, they have basically stopped saying anything at all. He has work and she has work and then the kids take up every spare ounce of energy she has. She used to make him wonderful dinners and greet him at the door in lingerie, and even though he knows that sort of stuff couldn't continue when the twins arrived, he thought he would be as in love, as involved with them, as she is. But he's not. He loves them, really loves them, but they're just too demanding. And boring. Kids are boring – a fact no one tells you. If he ever asks either of his sons about their day, the monologues on what happened in minute detail can go on for hours.

Rowan talks more than Sawyer but they both love to explain things to him the same way they do their mother, who is always ready to offer her rapt attention. 'So first I was being Mario and then I raced around the corner and kerunch off the side of the road and then woop, woop over and over and I crashed, pow, onto Sawyer who was being Princess Peach... and then he got mad and I...' Leo usually tuned out halfway through.

'Wait till they're teenagers,' Diana said when he asked her why the boys talked so much, 'they'll barely even speak to you – especially since you don't seem interested in what they have to say now.'

'I am interested,' Leo protested. 'Why do you always have to find fault with my parenting...' and the argument had gone on from there.

It had petered out soon enough. He and Diana can't even be bothered to argue with each other sometimes.

Yesterday morning, at the breakfast table, the twins had been arguing about one of the many video games they whiled away hours playing. They argued constantly about who was better at everything, from reading to soccer to brushing their teeth. 'I'm sure whoever finishes their breakfast first will get another ten minutes on the game,' said Diana wearily as she clutched a cup of black coffee in her hand.

Rowan and Sawyer both immediately stopped talking and wolfed down the last of their breakfasts, their cheeks bulging with toast as they stood at the same time.

'Done,' shouted Rowan, nearly choking on his last mouthful but not letting it stop him from dashing for his computer.

'Go on, you too,' sighed Diana and Sawyer followed his brother, shouting, 'I'm also getting ten more minutes.'

'You shouldn't do that,' said Leo. 'Computer games shouldn't be something that are a reward. They should finish and get ready without bribery.' He didn't look at Diana as he said the words but when he lifted his gaze from his phone, he could see that she was scrolling through Facebook, a small smile playing on her lips any time she saw something like a puppy or a kitten or a nice cake, her thumb moving back and forth as she liked everything. At least that's what he assumes she was looking at. He's never bothered to ask.

Leo finds himself at the front of the queue. He leans forward so the barman can hear him. 'Two double whiskies, thanks, mate.'

'Ice?' asks the young man as his hand moves to grab two glasses.

'Yes, he said he wanted ice, yes.' He doesn't know why he lies. Everyone is getting smashed on the free booze, everyone. No one is watching his consumption of two whiskies in a row.

With the glasses already chilling his hands, he turns to go.

'I hope one of those is for me,' says a woman and Leo stops, laughs and then he looks at her. His heart lifts. This day just got a million percent better.

'Of course it is,' he says, handing her a glass as his gaze roams down her body. The blue dress is tight over her hips and her waist looks so small he could wrap his hands around it. And her eyes, what do they call that? Ocean blue? Sky blue? Just amazing.

'Sure you wouldn't rather have a glass of wine?' he asks, and she offers him a dazzling smile and then she tips the glass up and drains the whole thing. He can see it goes down smoothly. There's no coughing or choking. This is a whisky drinker.

'Not really,' she says. Leo can't help laughing and then he does the same with his drink, the buzz from his last couple of drinks smashing into the new one, so voices are muffled and the room disappears and all he can see is long black hair and blue, blue eyes.

'I know you must be looking forward to the presentation from Jason Black this afternoon, but I thought I would skip it. I'm not sure how much I can learn from a lecture. I prefer one-on-one conversations. I like to really get to know people in the industry. Want to join me?' She leans forward and touches his arm and electric shocks trip through Leo's body.

'Absolutely,' he says, hoping he doesn't look like an idiot because he can't wipe the grin off his face.

'Leo Palmer,' he says, holding out his hand to shake hers.

'Serena Burns, commercial real estate,' she says, grasping his hand and making him woozy with her smooth skin and the smell of musky rose. 'We could go to the bar or we could just get some drinks in my room.' She licks her plump red lips.

Leo takes a deep breath, trying to control himself, trying to control his body. 'Your room,' he rasps.

'Come on then.' She winks and turns and he follows her, feeling like he's tethered to her.

He can't believe his luck.

# THREE

## DIANA

Five Weeks Ago

With the chicken casserole in the oven and the boys cajoled into homework with the reward of gaming time afterwards, Diana takes her tea into the living room and sinks into the sofa and the luxurious silence.

She does this every day, needing time to sit quietly and think through the day that is nearly over. Her patients at the clinic today run through her mind, starting with the mother who looked like she hadn't slept in days and the baby who was clearly not getting enough food. 'Breastfeeding is the goal,' she told her gently, 'but more important is a thriving bub and a happy mum. I think you're putting yourself under a lot of unnecessary stress.'

The woman burst into tears. 'I've tried so hard,' she cried.

Diana could see that she was both devastated and relieved. Devastated that she couldn't do what she wanted to do and relieved to have been given permission to stop trying. Diana advised her to come in again in a few days so they could see how things were going and she also told her to make an appointment with her GP and paediatrician.

She sips the chamomile tea and stares at the family portrait on the wall, hung above the television set.

Motherhood was so hard in the first months. Those early days with the twins are a complete blur of feeding and changing. Leo stayed home for a week and he was so good with them, great with them actually, but then she could feel him stepping back, removing himself back to his world and more interesting things.

They are a good-looking family. The professional photo shoot was a gift from her parents for their tenth anniversary and the pictures had turned out beautifully. It took ages to get Leo to commit to a time and at one point she was going to give up and just do one of her and the boys but she's glad she persisted. It's nice to have one of the whole family.

The boys have the same chestnut-brown hair and green eyes as Leo but their face shapes resemble hers. In the portrait, their personalities are so obvious, Rowan with a cheeky smile and Sawyer smiling but unable to conceal the dash of worry on his face. There was a bee buzzing around the photographer's head on the warm summer's day when they did the shoot in the park near the house. Sawyer was worried she would get stung.

They all look so happy, so perfect.

But nothing is ever perfect.

Right now, Leo is at his conference in Queensland, dressed in his best suit, his game face on. He will have enjoyed a long lunch and will have cocktail hour and a feast of a dinner to look forward to. And then, or maybe even before that, he will go back to his hotel room, but he won't go alone.

There will be someone with him.

And it's time for her to put a stop to it. To confront him and be done. The boys are old enough; her job is secure enough. It's time.

Four years ago, when he came back from a conference in Melbourne, he returned brimming with energy, holding flowers for her and overpriced bars of chocolate from the airport for the boys.

'What's this for?' she laughed.

'Just happy to be home,' he said.

And she knew. She arranged the flowers in a vase with her heart racing as she tried to convince herself that she was imagining it.

But later, when she collected his dirty laundry, the smell of another woman's perfume on his shirt confirmed it.

Her first reaction was shock. *How could this have happened to me? To us?*

But then she admitted to herself that her marriage was struggling; they were struggling and had been since the twins were born.

And then she was just exhausted at the thought of confronting him, of trying to figure out a way forward. She was in the middle of completing her postgraduate degree to be a child and family health nurse so she could work with mothers and babies. She barely had time to take a hot bath, let alone deal with the fallout of her husband cheating.

*It's just once,* she convinced herself. *I can forgive a one-time thing.* And because Leo had gone back to behaving exactly the same way he always did, she managed to make peace with her decision to let it go.

But then there was another conference and another one, and each time Leo returned with gifts, looking renewed.

And she kept forgiving as she finished her degree and found a job, all the while hoping that he wouldn't do it again. But he did and he will and she's done.

Leo is unhappy in their marriage. Diana knows this but cannot think how to help him because she spends a lot of time angry with him. He works long hours, ignores the boys who really want his attention, and seems to have lost interest in anything she has to say. She has a job but the entirety of their domestic lives falls on her, no matter how many times she asks for help. And she doesn't want to have to ask for help; she wants him to want to do his share.

'We should try therapy,' she told him over dinner a couple of months ago. 'I think it could be good for us.' She didn't want to give up without having tried everything. The boys would suffer and if she was going to put them through that, she wanted to be able to comfort herself with the idea that she had done everything she could to save their marriage. In therapy she could confront him about the cheating, force him to acknowledge it, and perhaps they could repair the damage?

'I'm not getting involved in that bullshit, Diana. We're fine.'

'Are we?'

'I don't actually have time for this conversation,' he said, standing and leaving the table. At the first sign of a real confrontation, Leo retreats to his office. She has said the words 'we need to talk,' only to be rebuffed so many times. *I have to run. We can talk another time. Let's just enjoy this dinner without getting into anything. Sorry, not now.* Perhaps Leo doesn't even hear them anymore.

Yesterday morning she had been looking at her phone, reading through posts on a divorce forum, gleaning advice from other women who have already been through what she knows is coming, and smiling despite herself at those who talked about how grateful they were to have changed their lives, how much better everything was now that the storm of divorce had blown over. Happiness in the future felt possible. She had been sitting right in front of Leo and he hadn't even noticed. And she wonders, if he had, would he even care?

They have lost each other but while she has found herself in her family and her work, he seems to have found himself in the company of other women. Fear and worry over being a single mother has kept her silent but she's not going to be silent any longer.

Leo can't be allowed to get away with what he's doing – not anymore.

# FOUR

## SERENA

Five Weeks Ago

'Happy?' Serena asks Leo and he nods, rubbing his eyes.

'That was amazing,' he says. 'You're amazing.'

Serena lays her head on his chest, listening to his heart pulsing through his skin, just a thin layer of skin and then flesh and bone. They had barely made it through the door of her hotel room before he was grabbing for her.

'Slow down, Leo Palmer,' she'd giggled. 'I need another drink.'

She had brought a bottle of whisky with her on the plane, chosen something expensive that he would probably recognise, and she had poured them each a large glass, drinking hers down quickly, swallowing a cough. She'd needed to be woozy, out of it, but still clear enough to remain vigilant.

She has always enjoyed whisky. At sixteen, on nights when she was up late working on an assignment or coming home from a night out with friends, she would often find her father in the living room, sitting in a small pool of light from the antique lamp on a side table next to the sofa, a whisky in his hand.

It was the way he processed the day. Silent sips in the near dark. Often, she would sit down next to him, just be in the silence with him, and he would offer her a sip. She liked the smell more than anything but, over time, she came to enjoy the taste. When he died, a year later, she took to sitting in his space, holding the glass he used to hold and drinking his whisky, just a mouthful, just enough to conjure his presence when the grief of his loss overwhelmed her. She was too young to be drinking and she didn't do it often but there was always enough whisky in the bottle and sometimes there was a new bottle as well.

'I can feel him here,' her mother said on mornings when the whisky smell permeated the air. But they'd never discussed it. Just a kindness they did for each other with no need for words. Serena forces her thoughts back to the hotel room, to where she is.

Sex with Leo had been better than she'd expected. She'd thought it would feel violating but he's considerate and he seems to have had the lecture on consent. 'Is this okay?' he kept asking.

She's relieved that the first time is over, that she's done what she came to do but now she just wants him gone.

Her legs are tangled up in the sheets of the hotel bed and her mascara stains the pillows. The whisky she downed swirls inside her, and she would like to stick her fingers down her throat and rid herself of everything. She would like to jump into a scalding shower and wash this man off her but she stills her body, taming her mind. *This needs to be done.*

Looking around the room, she notes that it's the perfect place for a hook-up with a stranger. There is nothing to distinguish it from any other hotel room in a large chain all over the world. Everything in the room is beige or brown, from the curtains to the carpet to the timber king-sized bed.

'When can I see you again?' asks Leo. 'Are you staying till tomorrow? Can we meet after dinner?'

Serena laughs. 'You're seeing me now.' She'll be long gone from this hotel before dinner.

Leo runs his hands along her bare skin, making her shiver. It's revulsion but he's not to know that.

'I really want to see you again before I leave. I know nothing about you but I do know I want to see you again. Where do you live?'

'Sydney,' she says and he smiles.

'Can I see you in Sydney?' he asks. He sits up, the sheet falling away from him.

At least he's a nice-looking man. He's in good shape for his age with tawny brown hair and green eyes. Feathered lines on his face make him look distinguished rather than old, and his stubble is perfectly trimmed and studded with grey. In another life she would be very attracted to him.

'Tell me about yourself,' he says.

'What would you like to know?'

'I want to know who you are. Where do you work? Are you married? Kids? I want to know everything. All I know right now is that you're in real estate and you like whisky.'

She didn't expect this from him. Not right away.

'And if I am married, do you feel bad about sleeping with a married woman? You're married.'

'How do you know? I'm not wearing a ring.'

She laughs. 'You look married,' she says, watching his face carefully. Does he believe her? That was a stupid mistake. Her muscles tense.

'Guilty, I guess.' He offers her a wry smile that he probably thinks looks cute. It doesn't. Serena won't let her mind wander to the woman waiting at home for Leo Palmer. He could have turned her down. He could have said, 'Actually I'm married, but thank you.' *Look how quickly he made the wrong choice.*

'Well...' she gathers the sheet around her and sits up, bringing to mind all the details she practised, 'I'm not married. I don't have an office because I work with high-end clients through word of mouth. I basically inherited the business from my father after he passed away. I keep everything very, very low-key but occasionally I come to these things just to see what's happening in the industry and it must be said' – here she licks her lips – 'there's always entertainment.'

'Where do you live in Sydney?' The eagerness in his voice is pathetic.

'Ah, ah.' She wags a finger at him. 'I want to see you again as well but I need to keep my work life and my personal life separate.'

'Whatever you want.' He sits forward, reaches for her and she moves away.

'Okay, good.' She smiles. 'I'll contact you when I get back. Maybe Tuesday?'

'Tuesday would be great.' He agrees eagerly.

'Book a hotel,' she says, 'a nice one. And I want to get lunch first.'

'Of course you do,' he says.

'Great, and now it's time to get back to work. Leave when I'm in the bathroom so I can get my head right for the rest of the day.'

Leo's laughter is loud and slightly sneering, making Serena flush, but she doesn't let it get to her. She watches him and waits for him to be done and when he's quiet, she drops the sheet and gets off the bed, picking up her phone and sashaying to the bathroom as he watches.

At the door to the bathroom, she pauses and turns to him, covertly snapping a quick photo of him in bed. 'You need to leave now or you won't see me again, simple as that.' She shrugs.

'But we still have lots of time left,' he protests.

'If you're still here when I get out of my shower, thanks, it was fun and I wish you a nice life. If you go, leave your number for me and I'll text you about next Tuesday.'

This is what she planned for too. Will he go along with it? She needs to maintain her distance, even as they get closer to each other. Serena Burns is aloof and in control.

She offers him one last smile and then she shuts the bathroom door and locks it, covering her hair and switching on the shower, stepping into the cold water. She waits for it to get hot, her body reacting to the temperature change immediately and washing away any other thought in her head.

He'll be gone when she gets out. She knows he will.

After fifteen minutes in the shower, she turns off the water and wraps herself in a large soft white towel. She is reluctant to open the door, to check if he's still there in case she has this all wrong.

Her phone vibrates in her hand and she looks down at the message she's received.

> *Please don't do this. You don't have to do this. There's another way to get what we want. The plan is working. I know it is.*

> **You hope it's working. You can't be sure. I need to get close to him. I can make him trust me and then this can all be over without anyone getting hurt.**

> *Maybe people should get hurt.*

> **Just give this a chance. Please.**

There is no reply. Serena deletes the texts and then looks at herself in the mirror. 'This needs to be done,' she whispers and then she allows herself a few tears before she straightens her shoulders and takes a deep breath. This is the way to do it, this is the way that no one gets hurt, that no one else has to suffer for what he's done.

Opening the door with agonising slowness, she is relieved to see the room empty, only the scent of whisky and the rumpled sheets evidence that anything happened here at all.

But something did happen and Serena knows this is just the beginning.

# FIVE

## LEO

Five Weeks Ago

He's never scrambled into his clothes as fast as he does when he hears the door of the bathroom lock.

It's after 5.30 p.m. and he knows he could go downstairs and wait for cocktail hour to begin but if he can't spend time with Serena, he wants to be alone. He wants to just relive the last couple of hours.

Before he leaves, he jots his number down on the writing pad provided by the hotel and adds a row of kisses underneath. Will she contact him? He's never had a woman give him instructions like this before. It's exciting; different. If it's a game she wants to play, he'll happily play. He'll do what he's told, if he can see her again. He'll book the hotel room tonight and hope like hell that she does call him. He knows the perfect place to take her. At the door, he pauses for a moment, wondering if she really wants him to stay even though she told him to go.

She doesn't seem like the kind of woman who says things she doesn't mean. She's smart and successful and she wants exactly what she wants. It feels like he's already just a little bit in love. Mind-blowing sex can do that to a person.

He leaves, checking the corridor first in case someone who may recognise him is out there but all is quiet, most of the agents probably still at the lecture by the great Jason Black on 'How to get the signature on the contract'. He can see them all there, their hands up as they ask question after question as though an answer from Jason Black will be some sort of blessing on their career.

Leo's glad to have missed it. He pulls his phone out of his pocket and takes a look at his messages. It's been on silent the whole day because he's left Robbie at the office to answer any queries from clients but there are a lot of messages from him.

Robbie has only been in real estate for a short time, having decided on a career change from being a carpenter. He's still learning but he's also thirty-four years old so, unlike the other young newly minted agents in the office, he gives off an air of having been in the game for a while. And he's good with clients, good-looking with blue eyes and a big smile. Leo can see that as soon as the young man has developed some confidence in the game, he'll make a lot of money, but right now he seems content to do whatever Leo needs him to do.

His messages over the last couple of hours have grown increasingly desperate.

> *Give me a call when you can. Need to chat re the Denton house.*

> *Hey Leo, let me know when you can talk, things going a bit pear-shaped re the Denton house.*

> *Hey Leo, we really need to chat about the Denton house.*

> *Leo, call me asap, thanks.*

Leo swears quietly under his breath as he makes his way to the lift so he can get to his own room, wishing he had the bottle of the smooth smoky whisky Serena had in her room to take with him. The buzz of incredible sex and whisky is wearing off quickly as he thinks about the Denton house.

He routinely goes out door-knocking in upmarket suburbs, letting owners know he's doing free appraisals in the area. Every now and again he gets lucky and that's what happened with Mrs Denton.

Her house is in a suburb currently on its way to gentrification as old red-brick houses are knocked down for large modern ones. The streets are wide and tree-lined, and on some streets, the harbour with its distinctive bridge can be seen in the distance. It means that the old houses are worth a lot for land value alone.

When he knocked on Mrs Denton's door, he knew she was a possibility as soon as she opened up and smiled at him. She's in her eighties and she lives alone and the house is falling to pieces around her.

He gave her his spiel about the price of land in her area going up and about how many houses he's sold in the last few months, stretching the truth just a little. He mentioned the huge amount of money she could expect if she was thinking about selling.

She stood and listened, nodding her head as he spoke, her pale-blue eyes widening when he talked about money. And then she invited him in and seemed happy enough to let him look around the living room.

'I've been here for fifty years,' she told him. Leo could see that the garden was overgrown, that the timber windows were rotting and that the whole house needed to be repainted or just demolished, and all he could think was 'ker-ching'.

'I've been thinking of leaving for a while but my grandson, Peter, said I shouldn't make any financial decisions without him. He's in the States and I hate to interrupt his work. He said that when he comes over in a few months, we'll talk about what to do about the house. I wouldn't know where to start.'

'What does he do?' Leo asked. The dusty surface of a large chest of drawers was covered in photographs of a baby growing into a boy and a young man and then a picture of that man holding a baby. Leo made a show of studying the photographs, even as he actually looked at the wall, studying the crack that extended to the ceiling.

'Oh, he's something very important, something to do with marketing,' said Mrs Denton, beaming with pride. 'That's why he said he would sort out the house.'

'Hmm,' said Leo, his foot moving over the worn, blue, flower-patterned carpet.

'Shall I make some tea?' she asked and Leo smiled.

'Tea would be lovely.'

'Sit, sit,' she said, waving at the grey sofa and Leo sat down, wondering how long this was going to take. He lifted his hands, trying to figure out some angles for photographs.

'Now where was I?' she asked when she returned with tea and a plate of chocolate digestives, biscuits that Leo hated but he immediately took one.

'You were telling me about your grandson,' said Leo.

'Yes, Peter. He's coming soon, I'm just not sure when.'

'And do you have any other children?' Leo asked. It was always good to know where the kids were, how many of them there were, exactly who might be interested in Mum selling her home. It never ceased to amaze him how much private information people were keen to share with someone who was willing to listen.

'Just the one. Peter's father. My son William is... was in prison,' she said, her tone dropping to a whisper over the terrible word. 'Drugs,' she said, even softer this time.

'That must have been very difficult for you,' Leo said, trying to visualise Rowan or Sawyer trapped in that kind of a life.

'It was,' she sighed, blowing her nose. 'He hurt someone and got sent to prison. It was after his father died. I was grateful for that, that my Thomas never got to see his boy in prison.'

'And where is he now?' asked Leo, taking another biscuit.

'I don't know... I thought he would come live here when he got out. But I don't even know when he was released. I just know his sentence was supposed to be for five years and that was seven years ago now.'

Leo nodded. There was more to the story but from what he could gather, the son was not in the picture.

Mrs Denton suddenly smiled. 'But Peter has been the light of my life.'

'That's so nice for you,' said Leo and he had to stifle a yawn. Other people's tragic stories were only of interest until he had the information he needed, which he did now. No son in the picture and a grandson in the USA.

He watched Mrs Denton's hand shake as she took a consoling chocolate biscuit.

'I do miss Peter,' she said after a sip of tea and Leo followed suit, wincing at the overly strong brew. 'But he said he'll be over for a visit soon, a few months from now, he said... I think... and as I said, he doesn't want me to make any decisions until he gets here.'

'I understand,' said Leo as he revved himself up for the sales pitch. 'I'm sure he wants nothing more than for you to be safe and happy and well taken care of. That way he wouldn't have to worry about you at all.'

'I don't like him to worry. He has such important work,' she agreed, nodding her head, and he knew he had her.

He took a brochure from his briefcase, glossy and colourful, filled with pictures of the elderly enjoying life to the fullest in landscaped gardens and beautifully decorated villas.

'If you sell, you could move somewhere like this where they have everything you could need,' he told her, handing her the brochure, watching her eyes widen at the Olympic-sized swimming pool and the library lined with books.

'They have great activities for seniors in all these complexes. And you know they say the market is turning with the interest rate rises so it would be good to get in quickly.'

She wasn't sure but he left the brochure with her, promising to call again.

It took a few visits over a couple of months, lots more strong tea and terrible digestives but eventually he persuaded her that a life of luxury awaited her. He even took her to see one of the villas for sale at a complex near her home, letting her marvel at how clean and modern and functioning everything was. It was the push she needed because all of a sudden, she was into the idea. And finally, he had the house on the market.

He had hoped the sale would go through quickly, had hoped that by the time the grandson came over from the USA, Mrs Denton would be safely ensconced in a nice little villa and the money would be in the bank and Leo could congratulate himself on a good sale.

He had possibly overpromised on the price and then the interest rate rises just kept coming every month and so offers had been a lot less than he'd hoped for. But when he'd got an offer he was happy with, he had just pushed her a little and she agreed to sell.

It wasn't Leo's fault that she was upset about that now. And it wasn't his fault that she couldn't actually afford one of the nice new villas in a retirement village.

The deposit had been paid and this whole experience should be over but it's not.

The Denton house had turned into a giant pain in the arse. But it had taken him too long and he had worked too hard to let it go. He should have known. Finding her before another agent did, had been extremely lucky and he's not even sure how it happened. Obviously, things were going to go pear-shaped at some stage.

In his hotel room he opens the small bar fridge, looks at the price of a tiny bottle of whisky. 'Screw it,' he says and opens the overpriced drink before he calls Robbie.

'Leo, God, why haven't you checked your phone?'

'Sorry, mate, I was in a lecture and I had it on silent. What's going on?'

'Mrs Denton called and said that she's changed her mind and doesn't want to sell. She says her grandson told her she'd made a mistake and that she was selling for too little and she needs to put a stop to the sale.'

'Yeah, well, that's not going to happen. She tried that with me a few days ago. It's not a big deal, Robbie; she just needs some reassurance that she won't get more for her crumbling pile of bricks and she'll be happy to go through with it. Just go over there and tell her that the market's dropped and you know, give her the whole talk.'

Robbie sighs and Leo clenches his fist. Robbie is just a little too nice and concerned about their clients. He needs to learn that it's a dog-eat-dog world in real estate. Jason Black never got anywhere being nice to people. He's as two-faced as they come, giving a box of expensive chocolates with one hand and handing you a contract before you've had time to think with the other.

'I feel bad about doing that,' says Robbie. 'She's really upset. Can't we just let it go? We can return the deposit. The buyer will cope.'

Leo rubs his face and glances at the fridge again. He should go downstairs and get something to eat and many, many more drinks.

'It's not a simple thing to get out of. I'll deal with it when I get back. Don't worry.'

'Okay, okay,' says Robbie, relief in his voice, 'but you may want to check your inbox as well. She told me that her grandson is going to email you and that he's planning a visit.'

'Yeah, he's always planning a visit but I haven't seen him yet – have you?'

'I guess not,' says Robbie sadly.

'I'll check for the email. Is there anything else?'

'No. Good conference?'

A ripple of excitement runs through Leo's body, reminding him of the afternoon he just spent with Serena.

'Really good, learning a lot. Next year you'll be here and you'll see.'

'Great,' says Robbie eagerly, 'I'll speak to you when you get back.'

'Yep, have a good night.'

Leo takes a deep breath and opens his emails, scrolls through looking for something that might be from Mrs Denton's grandson.

He finds it quickly enough – the subject heading is 'Arsehole'.

'Nice,' murmurs Leo as he opens it.

I want to be very clear with you, Mr Palmer. The sale for my grandmother's house is not going through. You took advantage of an old lady, incapable of making a sound decision. You pushed her into thousands of dollars of advertising for a house that needs a lot of work before it can be ready for sale. You promised her an outrageous price and then when it failed to sell, pushed her into a much lower price. There is nothing about what you've done that is acceptable practice in your business. I will not allow it to stand. I am going to be in Australia next month and I expect this entire problem to have been solved. I have already consulted a lawyer and will be moving forward with suing you if you do not get my grandmother out of this deal.

You are the worst kind of human being.
Sort it out!

Peter Denton

Leo reads through the email twice. Next month? By next month the house will be in the hands of the new owners and Leo will let everyone know that even though he gave Mrs Denton a chance to back out, she refused. She will refuse once he tells her how much money she'll lose or once he tells her that the house will be impossible to sell after this. Or that lawyers and the police might get involved – that's a good one. She'll sell. He'll make sure of that.

Standing, he drops his phone on his bed, looks over at the mirror and straightens his tie, slicks back his hair. And then he picks up the phone and deletes the email from Peter Denton. Screw him. This is not Leo's first rodeo.

He closes his eyes for a moment, reliving the afternoon with Serena and letting the image of her body push away all other thoughts. He's never taken one of his little dalliances back to Sydney where his family live. How will he keep it a secret?

*You've been pretty good at keeping secrets so far*, he tells himself as he smiles at his image in the hotel room mirror.

Things are looking up and he can't wait for next Tuesday.

# SIX

## DIANA

Five Weeks Ago

'And then... Dad, Dad, Dad, are you listening?' asks Rowan.

Leo looks up from his lap, where he is holding his phone. 'Yes, yes, I'm listening,' he says, obviously irritated. He wasn't.

'I'm sure Dad can't believe you were brave enough to hold the snake today,' says Diana, not wanting Rowan to realise.

'Yeah, that's great, Rowan. I'm not sure I would have been able to do that.'

'Well, Sawyer wasn't either,' says Rowan and Sawyer looks down at his plate.

'I didn't mind holding the lizard,' he says.

'I wouldn't have been able to touch either of those creatures,' says Diana, smiling. 'But now, boys, it's homework time.' The boys both spent the afternoon at soccer practice, which they do three times a week, loving the game with a fervour she would never have believed possible.

'We have to write about the reptile man coming to school today and then we have to write information about our favourite reptile so we have to use our computers,' says

Rowan, the important homework task demanding a serious tone.

'Well, I guess then you just have to use them,' says Diana, standing up from the kitchen table. 'But if I come upstairs and there is not a whole lot of research going on, I'm going to take away gaming time later, okay?'

'Only research,' agrees Sawyer. And both boys leave the kitchen.

'I hope homework is always this much fun,' says Diana as she stacks dishes into the dishwasher.

'Hmm,' says Leo, his eyes back on his phone.

'Good conference?' she asks. He has only just gotten back and it wouldn't have killed him to give the boys some undivided attention. He had arrived home with his usual gift of flowers for her and chocolates for the boys and a spring in his step. *Were you really expecting anything else?*

'Yeah, good, good,' says Leo, frowning.

'Something up?' she asks, making sure to keep her tone casual. Leo ignores her question.

'Meet anyone nice?' she tries and he looks at her, a small frown on his face.

'No one is nice; it's just a bunch of real estate agents, all trying to one-up each other. I see them at every conference.'

'So, no one new?'

'Why are you asking me all these questions? What exactly do you want to know?'

'I just wanted to know about your time away,' she says, taking his plate from in front of him.

'There's nothing to know,' he says, his eyes back on his phone.

'Well, I'd still like to know. Did you go to any good lectures?'

He keeps his eyes on his phone. Silence. He is even less interested in talking to her than usual and she wishes that it didn't hurt anymore, that she didn't have to see his gift of flowers as an indication of his guilt. *I have tried*, she thinks. *I have tried to change this but I can't.*

She concentrates on stacking the dishwasher as Leo stares down at his phone, muttering to himself. She wants to grab him and shake him, tell him to wake up and see what he's going to lose, but she keeps packing the dishwasher.

This morning she met with a lawyer; a woman named Jessica. 'Get your ducks in a row,' Jessica told her. 'Look into bank accounts, the deed for the house, everything. It's rare to start this process like you have, so take advantage of it,' she said, flipping her long blonde hair over her shoulder.

'What does that mean?' asked Diana.

'I mean you seem calm and in control, so make that work for you. I assume you haven't told him yet so make sure that when you do, you're in a position of strength. Most of the women who I see come in here at the end of their ropes. They're heartbroken and angry, very emotional with good reason. But it does mean that sometimes they are not looking at the things they should be looking at. Make sure he can't close the bank accounts, that kind of thing.'

'I am heartbroken,' Diana wanted to tell her, 'I just hide it well.'

'And if there are any skeletons in his closet – well... anything that can make him more pliable to negotiation. You want to have enough money to support your kids.' Diana stared at her and Jessica boldly met her gaze.

*Is this where we are now?* Diana thought. *Blackmail and the spilling of intimate secrets?*

'Do people really come in here and divulge their spouse's secrets?' Diana asked.

'You wouldn't believe the things I hear in this office,' she replied.

An image of Leo's desk at home and the locked drawer filled

with letters crossed her mind. One night last year, when the twins were being particularly recalcitrant about bed, Diana barged into Leo's office at home, surprising and startling him. 'I simply cannot deal with these boys tonight, Leo,' she said as he hastily dropped a letter into a drawer and then slammed the drawer shut.

'Who's that from?' she asked.

'No one, just junk mail,' he said as the boys thundered down the hallway on the second floor of the house, screaming about alien invaders.

'Can you please just deal with them, Leo?' she said, even as she watched him lock the drawer and shove the key in his pocket.

'Yes, yes, don't worry. Go and put your feet up.'

It was unusual for him to agree so easily. Diana had nodded her thanks and returned to the kitchen, listening as Leo went running upstairs. There was some laughing and then some yelling and then all was quiet and she breathed a sigh of relief.

The letter had slipped her mind until the next day when she was running the vacuum cleaner in his office. *No one puts junk mail in a locked drawer.*

She had hunted around his office but been unable to locate the key. She hasn't thought about the letter for some time but now, as she wipes down the kitchen counter, she wonders exactly what Leo is hiding and how she can get a look inside that drawer. Is it a letter from a woman? An old-fashioned love letter? How ridiculous.

She is surprised at a surge of jealousy that runs through her at the idea of another woman writing to Leo. That makes it more than just a conference fling and she wishes she didn't care at all. Does she still love him? She loves him as a father but he is less and less interested in the boys with each passing year. This year he has spent barely any time with them, pleading work whenever they have a soccer match.

She loves that he wants to provide for them, that he has allowed her to study to be a child and family health nurse and get her job at the clinic, despite its low pay.

They have been together for a long time and love is about shared history as much as it is about anything else. Despite making up her mind to leave her marriage, she finds she is still waiting for him to confess, for guilt to drive him into telling her the truth, and when he doesn't, it chips away at her soul. If he only has sex with women at conferences, can she just pretend she doesn't know? And what if it becomes something more? *Is he hiding a love letter or love letters? Is he in love, actually in love, with another woman?* Diana cannot bear the thought. Love and sex are different in a man's mind, or so she's read.

Her mother would encourage her to fight for her marriage because as she says, 'the worst marriage is better than the best divorce,' but Diana has fought in her own way. She has raised his sons and kept his house and let him get away with his vacations from real life. She has suggested therapy and tried to rekindle their early intimacy. And Leo just pulls further and further away.

Diana wanted to speak to Leo about a trial separation today but she has to admit, it makes more sense to wait. She will do as Jessica says and get her ducks in a row before she broaches the subject.

'Leo,' she says, looking at him as he types something into his phone, 'what's wrong? You seem really distracted.'

'I um... just a house sale. I had to go over to the woman who's selling and get her to accept that the sale needs to go through. It's the last thing I needed after getting off a plane this morning.'

'Why doesn't she want to sell?'

'It's a whole thing,' says Leo. 'I told her that the people who have bought the house love the area and they really want to build their dream home and that if she backs out, I can't guarantee that they won't get their lawyers involved and decide to sue her for not going through with the sale.'

'Can that happen?' asks Diana. 'I mean maybe she just changed her mind.'

'It can and I'm not going to take the fall for it. Don't worry, she agreed and it's a really nice commission. I didn't want to lose that. The school fees are expensive and the mortgage feels like it's growing instead of shrinking.'

'I understand but maybe you shouldn't push someone into a sale.'

'Diana, I'm not the bad guy here. I have a family to take care of. Just keeping the twins in soccer gear cost hundreds of dollars a year and your job doesn't exactly cover anything more than groceries and general living expenses. Between the mortgage and the car leases and school fees, it's... I needed the sale,' he sighs.

'Was she an older woman?' Diana asks, knowing that this would be the one person Leo would feel comfortable pushing like this and feeling guilty at the same time. She loves this house and she loves her job and she only wants the best for the boys. Leo does handle the lion's share of their expenses. Her mind jumps on the seesaw of *should I, shouldn't I* about the divorce. How much will she lose? How much will she gain and what will life be like for the boys? Because her loss is nothing compared to theirs. Leo sees little enough of them and he lives in the same house. What will happen if they're divorced?

'Old enough to know her own mind.'

'And her family?'

Leo waves his hand. 'Son in prison, grandson in the USA. He sent me a threatening email, but that was all bluff.'

'That sounds like a worry,' says Diana, finding a teabag to make herself a cup of tea. What exactly is Leo doing, pushing people into a sale? They don't discuss his work that often, except for him to tell her how busy he is.

'She was happy to go through with it after I talked to her, it's fine. I need to do some work so I'll see you in an hour or so,' he says.

He leaves her alone in the kitchen. The voices of Rowan and Sawyer drift downstairs and it's clear they are having an argument. She is weary at the prospect of going to sort that out.

'You both need to stop and just get on with the work or no gaming time tonight,' Leo shouts up the stairs and there is silence.

What will she do when she's alone and it's all on her? How exhausted will she be to have no one to help her ever? Leo's work means he is busy every Saturday so he's unlikely to be the sort of single father who takes his children for whole weekends. Even though he's not as interested in them as she is, it's nice to be able to tell someone when the boys succeed or when she is worried about them. She has her parents who adore their grand-children but no one can be a substitute for the father they both worship.

Her mind is back on the seesaw.

She should confront him. She should tell him she knows, but what if she does and he asks for a divorce? Is she ready, really ready to be on her own?

This has to come on her terms. She has to be in control of it or she won't be able to take care of her sons, the most important people in her world.

She goes upstairs and finds Leo's bag on the bed, pulls out the shirts and underwear that need to go into the washing.

Lifting his pale-blue shirt to her nose, she sniffs, hoping to only smell his aftershave but immediately catching the scent of another woman. *Is it the same woman as last year? Has he been meeting up with just one person all along, a person who sends love letters?*

'What are you doing?' she hears and she whirls around.

'Just seeing if this needed to be washed,' she says to Leo, who is standing in the doorway watching her.

He holds her gaze for a moment. 'I'm going to go for a run,' he says, coming into the room and shedding his clothes to change.

'Okay,' she says, something like despair in her throat.

He saw what she was doing and he didn't care. He didn't care at all.

# SEVEN

## SERENA

Three Weeks Ago

'Next week, same time, same place,' says Serena, sitting up in bed and then standing and walking to the bathroom. She walks slowly, letting Leo get one last look at her naked body. This is the third time they have slept together and she believes she only needs one or two more meetings before this is done. Each time they see each other, he wants to know when it can happen again. And each time they see each other she asks more questions about his life, delving deeper, trying to get him to open up to her. *What was your father like? What did you want to do when you were a child? What would you be doing if you weren't in real estate?* Leo loves these questions, loves her concentrated attention when he answers her.

In between, he likes to text her about his day, his thoughts about her, deals he's doing. He wants her to believe he's successful. He's eager to share his life with her. She shows interest but just enough to draw him in, just enough to keep him wanting to tell her everything he's thinking.

*Looking at a huge deal in the city, going to really put me on the
map. Maybe we could work together on something one day?*

**I don't think so. I work alone but I can't wait to
hear all about it.**

She doesn't know if his 'huge deal' is real or if he is postur-
ing. And some of the stuff he tells her over lunch makes her
squirm. It sounds like Leo will do anything to get a deal. He
even told her about bullying an old woman into selling her
home, not that he believes it was bullying. 'Sometimes sellers
need a bit of a wake-up call so they see the light. Everyone
believes their home is worth a fortune but I told her, "The
market decides what your home is worth and you made the
decision to sell, so trust the market."'

'And was she happy to "trust the market"?' Serena asked,
gesturing air quotes with her hands, as she experienced a twinge
of sympathy for the woman.

'Her happiness isn't my concern,' Leo replied. 'This is a
tough business, as you know.'

Serena hadn't replied to that, choosing to sip her wine
instead.

It surprises her how easy this is. No, not surprises... horrifies
her. This is not the kind of person she ever imagined she would
be. And yet she has an agenda and in order to fulfil that agenda,
this is who she has to be for now. This ability she has to separate
one part of herself from the whole amazes her. In this room,
with this man, she is Serena Burns right up until she steps into
the shower to wash him away.

This afternoon has been everything she expected it to be.
Lunch was perfect as they started with delicate cheese soufflés
and moved onto perfectly cooked steaks, pink and juicy and
paired with crispy roast potatoes.

'You parked downstairs?' she asked casually once they were seated.

'Yep, do you need a lift somewhere?' he asked, his voice high and hopeful.

'No, I'm good, thanks,' she replied. 'I may just pop to the ladies. Order a nice bottle of wine.' She stood up, and he saluted and smiled.

In the ladies, she took a deep breath and sent a text.

*His car is in the garage.*

**I can't believe you're going through with this again. I told you I had this handled.**

*And I told you we need another option.*

**I have another option that I'm prepared to use.**

*I don't want that for him or his family. It happened a long time ago and they don't need to pay for what he did.*

After all the discussions that have been had on how to do this, she's not backing out now.

She straightened her skirt and put on her best Serena Burns smile and left the bathroom.

As they ate their lunch, Serena looked around the restaurant and found herself unable to stifle a giggle at just how many couples there were.

'What are you laughing at?' Leo asked.

She leaned forward, gesturing that Leo should come closer so she could whisper her question. 'Do you think everyone here is sleeping with someone they're not married to?'

'Why do you say that?' he asked, looking around the room, oblivious to what she was seeing. The whole dining room seemed to be filled with older men and younger women. Was that why Leo had chosen the place?

'Have you done anything like this before?' she asked. If he couldn't see it, she wasn't going to bother explaining it.

'No, never.' *Liar.* 'I wish we could meet more often,' he said. 'I feel like we're really good together.'

'Leo,' she said softly, 'I like you but you're married.'

'I am, but it's...' he sighed, 'marriage is not a fairy tale. I feel like you and I have a real connection.'

She smiled. 'Like we could tell each other our deepest, darkest secrets.'

'Yeah,' he agreed, finishing up the last of his coffee.

'So, what's your deepest darkest secret, Leo Palmer?' she asked.

A smile played across his lips but at the same time his eyes looked wary. 'What's yours, Serena Burns?' he replied.

Serena shrugged. She needed him to trust her and it was clear they weren't there yet. That's fine. She would make sure they got there.

'Can I see you on Friday? I have a light day.'

'Sorry, no,' she said.

Leo frowned, a crestfallen little boy who wanted to stamp and shout, forcing Serena to placate him by running her shoeless foot up and down his leg. 'Every hour I spend with you lasts me a lifetime of days,' she said and he smiled, mollified as she had known he would be. He was so easy, so boringly easy. And it's because he's so easy that she is able to do this, able to be with a man in bed and separate herself from the experience completely. As soon as she sees him, she removes herself, her mind stepping away from where she is physically, the core of who she really is, safe from what she is doing. She has judged herself for this. Another woman's husband, and not just any man but this particular man. But her judgement is reserved for afterwards, for when she is alone again, and then she is able to give in to it and move through it and past it.

She grabs a towel from the bathroom and wraps it around herself, returning to sit next to him on the bed.

'Leo?' she says.

'Serena,' he answers, a grin on his face, stroking her arm lightly.

'How many times have you really cheated on your wife?'

His face changes and Leo swings his legs over the side of the bed, looking down to find his pants.

'Not gonna lie,' he says, 'I've had a few one-offs but never like this; never anything like this.' He stands and pulls on his pants.

'Do you think we're bad people?' asks Serena. 'I mean, people do a lot worse than this, don't they? People lie and steal and kill, so this is not so bad, is it? I mean I feel bad about this, all the time, but it's not really that bad, is it?'

She needs to open up to him so that he knows he can open up to her.

Leo's face darkens and then he says, 'I...' He stops, his grin reappearing. 'We're not so bad, Serena; no one is getting hurt from this.'

'Your wife?' she says, leaving the question hanging in the air.

'We don't need to discuss her. She and I have an under-standing of sorts. And what she doesn't know, won't hurt her.'

'True.' Serena smiles.

'Do you have a boyfriend, a husband?' he asks. It's not the first time he's asked this and each time she just smiles and shakes her head. When he asks it over text she stops answering. Who she has at home is none of his business.

'Why won't you tell me about your life?' he asks. 'I want to know everything.'

'Have you told me everything about your life?'

'You know a lot. Come on, just give me one thing.'

'Okay,' she sighs. 'I have a cat.'

'Nice, what's its name?'

'Mr Pickles,' she says, coming up with the name on the spot. She doesn't like cats. She's more of a dog person.

Leo laughs. 'No offence but you do not seem the type to name a cat Mr Pickles.'

'Well, we all have our quirks. Now tell me something about you? How old are your boys?' He's told her he has twin sons but she didn't push on their ages.

'Ten,' he says shortly. She's wandering into territory he doesn't like.

'It must have been hard when they were babies.'

He looks at her and then his eyes narrow and he looks away. There's something there he doesn't want to think about.

'It was,' he says.

'Back to work,' she says, knowing that she can't push anymore today, and then she stands up and heads into the bathroom.

Placing her phone on the slab of marble that holds two basins, she makes sure the water is scalding today and then she steps into the shower. She needs to clean away this whole afternoon.

When she gets out, he'll be gone.

So far, Leo has done things her way but it's only been three times. Will he figure this out for what it is or is he infatuated with her enough to not question anything?

He's hungry for information about her. He wants to know where she lives or where she works but she'll never give him what he wants. She'll share deals she's working on because he's in residential real estate and she is supposedly in commercial real estate but she won't tell him the name of her company or the address of actual properties she is working on.

She assumes he's looked her up but all he will be able to

find is a LinkedIn profile and that has precious little information. She's told him she works for herself with high-end clients
and no official office. 'I know a lot of people,' is all she has said
and even though it's possible that if he thought about any of the
things she says, he would know that she's built a cocoon of lies
around herself, he's never said anything. He doesn't push or
question. He's too afraid of losing her and their afternoons of
pleasure, of losing her attention. Stupid man.

She's instructed him to never mention her. *If I hear you've
been asking about me – and let's face it, the real estate game is
not exactly huge here in Sydney – it will be the last time we see
each other*, she told him when she texted him to meet her in
Sydney for the first time.

When she steps out of the shower, she wraps a fluffy white
towel around herself and checks the room. Leo is gone, just a
faint lingering scent of his tart aftershave.

Serena uses her make-up remover to clean her face,
removing false eyelashes as well. She pulls off the irritating
fake nails painted in a deep red and then she removes the
blue-coloured contact lenses from her eyes, blinking rapidly as
she studies her brown eyes in the mirror. It's the removing of a
filter, of a lens through which she wants to be seen right now
and there are moments when she wishes she could hold tightly
to that lens. Serena Burns is so much bolder than she is.
Finally, she works at the wig, using rubbing alcohol to
painstakingly remove the glue and experiencing a rush of
relief when she can finally pull it off. She would take it off
immediately, before she gets in the shower, but she is always
worried about him still being in the room. She rubs her fingers
through her light-brown hair, bringing sensation back to her
scalp. The wig is very tight and attached securely because she
can't risk it coming off. She tries to steer his hands away whenever he gets near her head. The wig is made of human hair
and it was very expensive but it's worth every penny. She

doesn't even recognise herself in the mirror when she has it on.

She dresses in the clothes she has in the bag she brings, pulling on a pair of faded jeans and an old T-shirt and baggy jumper against the cool air outside. Looking in the mirror, she brushes her hair and ties it back into a neat high ponytail.

And then she takes a few deep breaths, settling back into who she is. There is no sound in the blessedly silent room except the low hum of the air conditioner, warming the space. The bed is a mess of rumpled sheets; the smell of sex lingers in the air.

She waits another half an hour, watching a sitcom on television just so she can be absolutely sure that he's gone but even then, she checks the corridor carefully before leaving the room, and she pulls a baseball cap onto her head. She walks quickly and is soon out on the street in the cold, the air rushing around her as she heads for the train station.

Serena wore a red pencil skirt today with a blouse in cream with a plunging neckline. The clothes are hers at least, from a time when she worked in the city instead of where she works now.

She's only twenty-eight but her career in advertising had never felt right and at twenty-five she had found herself unable to contemplate another day of trying to sell unnecessary products to the world at large by telling those watching or listening or reading that they were too fat or too thin or too smelly or too old.

She had taken herself back to university to study nursing and now she works in a care home, with a mix of the elderly and young adults with special needs. It's demanding work, sometimes heartbreaking but also filled with moments of joy as she cares for those who cannot care for themselves.

Her mind runs through the list of patients she's worried about, including Mr Evans who is moving less and less but refusing physical therapy, and Mrs Rose, who is still waiting for her family to pay her a visit after two months. The world is filled with despicable people and Leo Palmer is probably up there with the worst of them. The very worst of them.

Once she's on the train, she finds a seat alone and settles in for the forty-minute journey back to her suburb.

And then she takes a deep breath and sends another text. To a different number this time.

*Want to know a secret?*

'Here we go,' she whispers aloud, glad no one is sitting near her. 'Here we go.'

# EIGHT

## LEO

Three Weeks Ago

He walks down to his car slowly, holding on to the electric buzz of good food and great sex running through his body. He wouldn't have minded a nap, would have loved to have her lying beside him as they slept, but Serena has rules and even though he keeps trying to get her to break them, he actually finds them exciting. She's so in charge, so bold. They discuss real estate over lunch, meander into politics and the news. She's smart and interesting but they both know everything is just a prelude to the sex.

Checking his watch, he sees it's after 3 p.m. and he hurries to his car, clicking the alarm.

His left hand moves towards his door handle as he swings his briefcase into his right, and then he stops. He takes a step back away from his bronze Porsche Macan, just expensive enough to prove his success to clients but still cheap enough to afford the payments, and stares at the damage.

Shaking his head, he walks around the beautiful car, following the deep gouge in the metallic paintwork that covers every panel. Someone has not just keyed his car, but taken what looks like a blade to it. He looks around the parking garage that is located under the hotel, seeking out cameras.

There's a camera at the top of the row he's parked in. He wants to sit down and cry at the damage, actually cry. Diana hates this car, hates how much it costs them every month, especially in the months when he sells nothing and has no commission to look forward to, but he had insisted he needed it.

Striding purposefully towards the security office at the front, he feels his body heat up with rage. This is supposed to be a secure parking lot. What kind of an operation are these people running? There's no way he's going to get his insurance to pay out and cop the excess, no way.

The office is basically a small glass box and Leo can see a young man slouched on a chair inside, his gaze on his phone.

Leo raps on the door and opens it, startling the man who looks no more than seventeen with scruffy bits of beard clinging to his chin.

'Jeez, you scared the crap out of me,' he says.

'Listen,' says Leo, 'someone has keyed my car, the whole thing. Not even just keyed, it looks like they've used a blade.' He struggles to keep himself from yelling. 'I thought this was a secure parking lot. What's going on here?'

The young man stands up, shoving his phone into his pocket, and runs his hands through his unruly bleached white hair. 'That's not good,' he says.

'Yeah, I know,' says Leo. 'I need to see the security cameras. I want to see who did it.'

'Um,' says the young man, his eyes darting from side to side, 'the ones at the front and the exit work but... yeah, not all of them.'

'You're kidding me, right? My car was damaged in your parking lot. Get the manager down here.' He squeezes the handle of his briefcase, resisting the urge to swing it at the boy and batter some sense into him.

'Um, okay, okay, just like calm down. I'm gonna call him.'

Leo bites down on his lip, wanting to shake the boy by his shoulders as he watches him pick up a phone and make a call.

Ten minutes later, Leo has paced up and down the row where his car is parked so many times, he thinks he may be going crazy. Finally, a man who looks about Leo's age appears, his grey hair slicked neatly back, his suit a perfect shade of navy blue. A simple, elegant nametag reads *Silas – Manager* in neat black lettering.

'I believe we have a problem,' says Silas smoothly, as though he doesn't know exactly what the problem is.

'We do,' says Leo, and he walks towards his car with the manager following him.

'This was done in your car park,' he says, pointing to the damage, 'and I want to know what you're going to do about it.'

'Are you sure it happened here?' asks the man, his voice oily with condescension. 'Rodney would have seen if anyone who was not supposed to be here walked in.'

'Rodney seems more interested in his phone,' says Leo, 'and he told. Me. The. Cameras. Are. Broken.' He spits out each word separately as Silas gazes at him.

'Well,' says Silas, turning briefly to look back at Rodney who has helpfully followed them and is now watching them speak with his hands shoved in his pockets, 'even though some are non-operational, I can assure you that only guests of the hotel are in this car park and it's not... I mean we've never had anything like this happen before. Perhaps you simply didn't notice it before?'

'Who would miss this?' yells Leo, gesturing towards his car.

'I'm sure I don't know,' says Silas, folding his hands together. 'If you're staying at the hotel for a few days, I will absolutely look into it and we can summon the police as well.'

Leo thinks about getting the police involved, thinks about the questions he may be asked about what he is doing at a hotel in the city on a Tuesday afternoon and the repercussions of Diana finding out about anything. He caught her sniffing his shirt when he got back from the conference a couple of weeks ago. Does she suspect something? Know something? The last thing he needs right now is to be accused of cheating. The situation feels precarious, like it could easily become something that results in more damage to his life than just the damage to his car.

'The police could be here in just a few minutes,' says Silas helpfully.

Leo knows his excess is a thousand dollars. For a thousand dollars he can get the car fixed and lie about where it happened but if the police interview him, if the police come...

'Never mind, I don't have time for this crap. You need to fix your cameras,' he huffs.

'Of course, sir, but it won't take long to summon the police,' says Silas, and Leo can see a slight twitch at the corner of the man's mouth. It's clear that the manager knows his time at the hotel is not something Leo wants to discuss. Perhaps this is affair central and greasy Silas knows this.

'I'm late for an appointment, but if you think I'm paying for parking in a place where my car was damaged, you're wrong.'

'Absolutely,' says the manager. 'Rodney, please go and open the boom gate for Mr...?'

Leo doesn't reply, just climbs into his car and gets the hell out of the parking lot, fury whizzing around his body.

He spends the drive back to work hating Rodney and his slimy manager and the hotel, the afternoon of great sex disappearing and his usual low mood at how ordinary, how plodding his life has become, returning.

Who would do that to his car? Emails from disgruntled clients run through his head but no one he thinks he needs to worry about. Peter Denton, perhaps, but the man is safely tucked away in the USA.

Maybe it's something to do with Serena, and he allows the idea of her actually having a boyfriend to creep into his mind. She's always denied she has but what if she's lying? Well, not really denied it but she shakes her head when he asks her. He finds it unbelievable that she doesn't have a boyfriend when he's sure men her age would be lining up to spend time with her. Is she lying by omission? She doesn't answer the question so he's assumed it's a 'no' on the boyfriend front but maybe it's just a 'I'm not going to talk about him' shake of the head. It's possible that Serena is in some kind of complicated relationship and Leo's car has just paid the price for that.

When he has parked outside his office, he texts her quickly. She is saved in his phone under the name Jeremy-Strata plumber and he immediately deletes any texts between them.

*Someone damaged my car at the hotel.*

He waits for five minutes, his eyes on the large window into the office where he can see Robbie flirting with the new receptionist, a young woman with curly blonde hair and big blue eyes and the improbable name of Blake.

She responds, *Poor baby*.

*No one knew I was there except you.*

**Are you suggesting I keyed your car?**

Leo can feel her laughing at him.

*No, obviously not but you keep saying there's no one else in your life and now I'm wondering...*

*If I have a psychotic boyfriend who followed me to the hotel?*

*Yes, you've never said yes or no. I'm wondering if there is someone who is not happy about our relationship.*

Leo can feel time moving forward second by second as he waits for her reply. He's made her angry. He's sure he's made her angry. He should not have sent the last text. 'Idiot,' he curses himself aloud.

*Firstly, I wouldn't call what we have a relationship, and secondly – are you sure someone isn't just upset with you, Leo? Someone who you may have hurt?*

Leo sighs. Who could be angry enough with him to do that to his car? A former client? His wife?

*I think a boyfriend of yours is the more likely scenario.*

Again, he waits, time passing while he gnaws on a nail.

*I'm more than happy to end this if you think I'm lying and we can both move on with our lives.*

Leo's heart races at that idea, at the terrible weeks and months that loom ahead of him with the endless repetition of days and no Serena.

*No, of course I don't think you're lying. It's just weird.*

*Life really isn't fair, poor love xxxx*

Something about the reply makes Leo uneasy but he doesn't have the energy to examine the feeling. At least she didn't say things were over.

He needs to do some work and so he reluctantly replies with a few kisses of his own and deletes the messages, hoping that Serena is doing the same thing.

Leo climbs out of his car and takes another look at the damage. It's even worse in the bright July sunlight in the parking lot in front of the real estate agency. Who would do something like this to him? He's never hurt anyone.

Even as he thinks this, a list of upset clients, angry ex-girl-friends and assorted people runs through his head. Maybe 'never' is not quite the word he's looking for.

Sighing, he walks into the office.

'Did you get the listing?' asks Robbie when he sees him and Leo thinks fast, trying to recall what Robbie is talking about, and then he remembers that he told Robbie he was going to see someone on the northern beaches about the sale of their big old house.

'I have the golden touch so it's nearly in the bag,' he says.

'Good man,' laughs Robbie. 'We need a big one.'

'Yeah,' agrees Leo and then he goes into his office and closes the door, his whole wonderful afternoon disappearing.

Opening his computer, he checks his personal inbox and sees two separate emails from Peter Denton in the USA. Prickling unease creeps through Leo. The first email from Peter Denton came to his work email. But this is the email address he uses for his personal life. It wouldn't have been hard to find, but still. Why has Peter Denton messaged him on a different email address? The contact feels more threatening.

You are not going to get away with this, Leo Palmer. You pushed my grandmother into a sale and when I get there,

you will be sorry. This is malpractice. This is bullying and
fraud.

It's followed by a second email as though Peter Denton just
couldn't contain his rage long enough to just send out one well
thought-out message.

You're a sick bastard. If you think you can bully an old lady
into a sale and get away with it, you're wrong. You have no
idea who you're dealing with, Leo Palmer.

Leo wants to laugh off the emails, especially since the guy
keeps referring to him by his full name, like some kind of old-
time gangster. But then he thinks about his car and the damage.
Maybe Peter Denton has friends in Australia who are willing to
damage a car for him. But how would anyone have known
where he was?

What if Peter Denton is already in the country and is
following him around?

Did Peter Denton gouge his car?

He checks the email address but he has no real idea what
he's looking for. Is the email from the US or not? Could he ask
Robbie to try and trace it; he seems like he might know how to
do something like that. All the younger generation do.

Leo stands up to go and get Robbie so he can ask how to
trace the email but almost immediately he sits down again. He
can look up how to do it himself and he doesn't really want
Robbie seeing these emails. He told Robbie that Peter Denton
was not a problem.

He's not going to deal with this now. Leo deletes the emails.
If the damage to his car is related to this in any way, maybe it's
done now. If the guy is in the country and following him,
perhaps that's the worst thing that he's going to do. Leo will

suck it up and pay the excess, lie about where it happened and move on with his life.

He turns his black leather swivel chair to look out of his window at his beautiful damaged car in the parking lot. It could have been someone else, just a random person who hated the idea of anyone owning a luxury car. Swivelling back to face his desk, he decides that he's not going to let this worry him at all. If Peter Denton turns up here, that's a worry but otherwise the man is probably just firing off emails from the USA and will do nothing once he gets here.

It's also easier to decide he's been the victim of some ugly prank by some weirdo in a parking lot. Maybe Rodney was tired of his job... anything is possible. He's not going to think about that either.

Taking a deep breath, he opens his work emails, congratulating himself on his ability to push aside things he doesn't want to or need to think about. He needs to just keep moving forward and everything will be fine. Like a shark. Leo pulls his shoulders back and conjures the image of a deadly shark, letting it inspire him to get on with his work.

Serena pops into his head again and he closes his eyes, thinks about the feel of her skin under his fingertips. She's agreed to meet again so at least he has that to look forward to.

# NINE

## DIANA

Three Weeks Ago

It's after 9 p.m. by the time the kitchen is clean and the boys are in bed. Leo is in his office downstairs. 'Busy, busy, busy,' he told her, disappearing in there without even eating dinner. She left him something in the kitchen. He'll eat when they've all gone to bed.

He's angry with her.

He arrived home full of fury over the damage to his precious sports car and she hadn't responded correctly.

'It's your own fault for driving such a ridiculously expensive car, Leo,' Diana said as she surveyed the damage after he made her come outside and look at it.

'Yeah, I thought you would say that. You know why I need to drive this car, Diana. I have an image I need to project.'

'It didn't need to be a Porsche,' said Diana, folding her arms. She hated the ridiculously expensive car, hated that it cost so much to maintain and that he would never let the boys in it because they might mess up the interior.

'So you're saying that it's actually my fault my car got damaged?'

'Where were you anyway?'

'It was in the street when I was seeing someone for a property appraisal. I was actually doing my job, Diana, and someone vandalised my car.'

'What street?' she asked, sceptical. It was cold in the driveway with a winter storm threatening.

'I can't remember. I did a lot of appraisals today.'

'I thought you usually spent Tuesdays in the office.'

'Well, not today. Are you keeping track of my movements? That's weird.'

'No, Leo,' she sighed, 'I just listen when you talk.'

'Yeah, well, I did some today and I can't remember which street I was on.'

'What do you mean, you can't remember? You must remember the street where the damage happened. You must have been furious. I would have been. And lots of houses have cameras now. Maybe someone's camera caught the vandal in the act. You need to go to the police. You can't just accept this.'

'I don't want to make a big deal of this, Diana. I just want to get it fixed.'

'What has gotten into you, Leo? You're going to have to pay the excess and we can ill afford a thousand dollars right now, especially since all your "appraisals",' she said, using her fingers to indicate air quotes around the word 'appraisals', 'don't seem to be leading anywhere right now.' She didn't really believe that's what he'd been doing. He was probably having a long lunch somewhere. She was being nasty and she knew it but she didn't care. The damage was going to cost a fortune to fix.

'Whatever,' Leo replied, walking away from her and back into the house.

Diana takes her phone upstairs and runs herself a bath, filling it with rose-scented oil. The large tub is her favourite luxury. She rarely has time to use it and she should just go to sleep but she needs something nice to end her day.

Slipping into the warm water and picking up her phone, she scrolls through missed text messages that have come in while she's been working. There's one from her mother, *I've booked the Mexican restaurant Dad likes for his birthday next month. The boys love it so it's good for everyone. Sunday lunch. Let me know if Leo will be joining us.*

There's one from the young mother she advised to give up breastfeeding, *Thank you so much, he slept for four hours in a row last night!!* Diana smiles. She loves it when she can help.

There are text messages from clothing stores advertising specials and then one from another nurse at the clinic asking about coordinating vacation time. Something she can deal with tomorrow. She keeps scrolling and then she stops at a message from a number that she's never seen before.

*Want to know a secret?*

Spam? A scam? She stares at it, tries to memorise the number to google it but nothing comes up. Maybe a store trying to lure her in? She clicks on the message but it's just the message.

She should just delete it but something is stopping her from doing that.

Her thumb hovers over her screen. Finally, she sits up, immediately cold once her body is out of the warm, fragrant water.

*?*

It seems the safest reply.

She puts her phone down and slides into the water again. Whoever it is, won't reply. It's probably some sort of joke.

She closes her eyes and takes a deep breath and as she breathes out, a message comes in.

Grabbing the hand towel next to her, she dries her hand and picks up her phone. They replied and it's an image. She debates over clicking on it. It will probably infect her phone with a virus. She puts the phone down and then immediately picks it up again and clicks on the image before she can talk herself out of it.

It's her husband. It's Leo.

Leo, lying in what is obviously a hotel bed, the sheets rumpled around him, bliss on his face.

It doesn't need an explanation.

Diana drops the phone, slides right under the water and opens her mouth, screaming with everything she has into the soapy tasting water.

It's her husband.

She closes her eyes, holds her breath, stays under the water.

His vacation from real life has somehow found her. How? She thinks about all the places where her number is listed. It's on the clinic website.

THE CLINIC IS OPEN FROM 9 A.M. TO 3 P.M. IF THIS IS AN EMERGENCY, PLEASE CALL 000. IF YOU HAVE AN APPOINTMENT AND THE DOOR IS LOCKED, PLEASE CALL DIANA ON...

Her number is listed because sometimes she is alone at the clinic and it feels safer to have the door locked. There's a bell but her number is there in case she doesn't hear it. Rarely, very rarely, she gets a call from a mother who needs some advice late at night. Occasionally she's been sent images of a thermometer with a temperature reading and a desperate text: *should I go to the hospital???*

New mothers panic easily. Even Diana, with all her nursing

knowledge from her job as a midwife, remembers panicking when both Rowan and Sawyer got ear infections at the same time and both their temperatures passed 39 degrees. It's one of the reasons she did the postgraduate degree in child and family health. She wanted to help after the baby was born. She wanted to be there for new mothers, those breezing through the first few months and those struggling.

When the twins were sick, Leo had rushed to the hospital with her, both of them terrified at the sight of their pale, subdued infant sons.

How things have changed.

Now he is pictured in a hotel room bed after sex with someone else.

She needs to breathe, can hear her heartbeat in her ears, her lungs are beginning to burn.

She sits up again, water sluicing off her body as she takes a deep gasping breath. She runs her hands over her hair, her body hot and cold all at once. And then she lifts her knees and curls her arms around them, rocking back and forth in the bathwater. What does she do now? What now?

She tries to channel the woman who was at the lawyer's office only two weeks ago, to find that calm, in-control, somewhat numb person. What should she do now? How does she play this?

Drying her hands again, she looks at the bathroom door, is relieved that she remembered to lock it. She picks up the phone and texts back.

**You obviously want to talk, so let's talk.**

She sits in the bath, staring at the phone until the water grows cold and her fingers prune but there is no reply.

Eventually she gets out, wrapping her body and her hair in towels and then she sits on the edge of the tub, looking at the picture of Leo in a hotel room after sex with another woman. He looks so happy.

He is looking right at the person taking the picture. There is such contentment on his face. She can remember when he used to look at her like that.

'To my stunning, clever, funny, compassionate and kind wife, thank you for agreeing to marry me,' he had said when he'd toasted her at their wedding.

Was it just having children that changed everything? All her friends had children and their husbands didn't stray – at least she assumes they don't. Leo seems to have some kind of hunger in him, some need for a bigger life. He was a star in real estate when they met but then somewhere along the way, around the time the twins were starting to crawl and sit, something changed. He changed. He started to lose sales, to falter. He pulled himself back on course but he still seems to view their life as less than. He's not making the money he thought he would be by now. He compares himself to everyone else in the business. He is hungry for something she can't give him. So, he goes to other women.

Anger rises inside her. She will show him this picture now, confront him and tell him to leave. She stands and opens the bathroom door. Leo is still downstairs in his study and she hastily pulls on pyjamas and a robe, tying her wet hair back. In the mirror she can see the shadows under her eyes, the wrinkles around her mouth. She's older but so is he. Arsehole. How could he do this to her, to their family?

Clutching the phone in her hand, she goes to leave the bedroom when another message comes in.

*He's not the man you think he is.*

Diana doesn't even think about whether or not to reply, she just types.

*Clearly. What do you want?*

*I think you should know who he is and what he's done.*

*He's cheated on me. And by the looks of this picture, you must be the woman he's cheated with.*

*There's more than that.*

*What more?*

*It's a long story. It goes back years. Can we meet?*

Diana feels like she can see a swirling red light above her head, like she can hear sirens and the word, 'danger, danger, danger,' all around her.

If she is going to go ahead with the divorce, then she needs all the ammunition she can get.

Leo makes more money and he will be angry. He will deny cheating. He will deny everything unless she has proof.

*How can we meet? Don't you live interstate?*

*I live in Sydney.*

Diana's heart is heavy in her chest. A hook-up at a conference is one thing but now he's brought his affair home with him, home to the state she and her children live in. Has she always lived here? Has he been seeing her all along and has she been sending him love letters that he keeps and reads over and again? Is he downstairs thinking about her right now in their family space? The thought disgusts her.

*When?* Diana asks.

*End of next week,* comes the quick reply.

**Why not tomorrow?**

*End of next week,* is repeated.

Diana doesn't know how she will survive the wait, how she will keep herself from asking Leo about this, how she will keep functioning.

*It needs to be sooner,* she texts.

*End of next week.*

Diana would like to throw her phone against the wall but she squeezes it tightly instead. She will have to wait. She will practice patience and she will wait.

*Fine,* she replies and then she texts a place to meet, not letting the woman make her own suggestion.

Whoever this woman is, she has something to say about Leo.

And even though she doesn't want to hear it, Diana knows she has no choice.

The next morning, after Leo has left for work, Diana takes advantage of the fact that she has a late start and goes into Leo's office, determined to find the key for that locked drawer. She hunts around, opening and closing other drawers and the filing cabinet, moving everything carefully and putting it back just the way she found it, but there's nothing. Determined, she tries again and eventually she opens a drawer in the filing cabinet and runs her hands under the files, across the bottom of the drawer.

Her fingers touch metal, and she slides the object along the bottom of the drawer until she gets a hold of it.

With trembling hands, she slides the key into the lock and opens the drawer. It's difficult to move it at first and she realises that it's stuffed to the top with letters.

She gives the drawer a pull and stares down. There must be at least fifty letters, maybe more. Diana lifts one up. Her heart races as she reads Leo's PO Box address on the front and then the address on the back. *Long Vale Correctional Facility.* The letter isn't opened. This is not a love letter.

She picks up another one but it's still sealed as well. She goes through all of them.

'Just a bloody minute, okay, I left the file at home,' she hears and her heart leaps into her throat. She slams the drawer and then stands, shoving the key back into the cabinet.

The office door opens.

'What are you doing here?' asks Leo, real anger in his voice.

Hoping that she can keep her voice steady, Diana says, 'I was just looking for a stapler. I can't find mine.'

Both of them stare down at the stapler on Leo's desk.

'I really need a coffee,' she says, smiling and picking up the stapler and walking out of the office.

In the kitchen, she makes herself a cup of coffee, her third one of the day, as a thousand questions run through her mind.

The second she saw the name of the prison she knew who the letters were from. But why are they being sent to Leo?

And why hasn't Leo opened a single one of them?

# TEN

## SERENA

Two Weeks Ago

> *I'm so sorry. I have to cancel tomorrow. Something's come up*
> *at work.*

Serena sends the text and waits.

Leo is at his office. His damaged car stands in the parking lot, the gouges glinting in the sun.

Serena is standing outside the agency in front of the parking lot with a coffee in her hand. She has stuffed her hair up into a baseball cap and pulled it down over her face. Her eyes are obscured by oversized sunglasses and a long black puffer jacket covers her body. She is gazing at the window of the agency where beautiful houses for sale are pictured in their best light. Her heart races at the idea that, any moment, Leo may appear and demand to know what she's doing here.

Leo's office faces the parking lot and even though his chair is in front of his large glass window, its back hiding most of his body, she can see him. Even through the myriad of real estate choices she can still make out the dark blue of his suit as he reaches for things on his desk. For a moment she studies a picture of a four-bedroom home with a large garden carpeted in bright-green grass and imagines a future for herself where such a thing would be possible. She cannot picture a time after this is done, cannot see herself moving on with life and maybe getting married and having children.

She is close enough, pretending to study the listings, that she almost believes she has heard the ping of the text being received.

She shouldn't be here. Instead, she should have sent the message from home or from her car or from the care home where she's due in twenty minutes, but she wanted to watch his reaction. Craved his reaction, his disappointment, his anger. There is something about this subterfuge that has drawn her here to see him in his day job being Leo the real estate agent and family man. Perhaps she is hoping to get caught because then it will be over and she can go back to being herself? Perhaps she is hoping to see something of him that will make her reconsider what she's doing?

In his office, Leo reaches for his phone on his desk and reads the message. Serena holds her breath.

The office chair is shoved roughly back and Leo stands and then whirls around to face the window. Serena's heart leaps in her chest and for a second she is frozen on the spot but then she darts out of sight, around the side of the building.

The cup of coffee shakes in her hand as she breathes in and out slowly. She holds her phone in her hand, waiting for his reply.

**That's fine. Work comes first.**

Serena smiles. A message without the kisses he usually sends. Good.

'Can I help you?'

Serena spins around to find herself staring at a young blonde woman dressed in a short, tight grey skirt teamed with a cream blouse and grey waistcoat. Her arms are folded and she is holding a cigarette in one hand. She bounces up and down on her toes, keeping warm in the winter wind as she inhales her cigarette in one long breath, letting the smoke float out into the air, the smell heavy and thick but not unpleasant.

'Oh, no, thanks, I was just... looking for something to rent and I felt a bit... I needed a moment,' Serena says to the young woman. She's not a good liar unless she's prepared. She reaches up and pulls the peak of her cap further down over her face.

The woman smiles and ashes her cigarette on the ground as Serena watches her. 'I know, the prices of rentals these days is enough to make you lose your mind. I don't think I'm ever going to be able to move out of home and my mum drives me mad.'

'Oh,' Serena answers, unsure how to respond to this confession.

'Sorry, bad day.' The woman laughs lightly. 'I'm just saying I know what you're feeling. Everything is completely over the top and I work in a real estate agency, so I should know.'

Serena sighs, relief oozing through her body at the woman's understanding and acceptance of her strange behaviour. 'Everything is very expensive.'

The woman draws on the cigarette again, and then she drops it on the ground and grinds her heel into the butt. 'Robbie is inside and he deals with a lot of rentals. He's just starting out in real estate but he's a lovely bloke. I can introduce you and you can tell him what you're looking for and what you have to spend. He always goes above and beyond for people.' The blonde woman smiles and flushes a little.

'I bet he's nice-looking too,' says Serena and the woman giggles.

'Want to come inside with me?'

'Oh, no... I have to get back to work.'

'Blake, are you out here?' they hear, and a man comes around the corner. 'I knew you were sneaking a ciggie out here,' he says before registering Serena. 'Oh, sorry,' he says. 'I didn't realise you had company.'

'Just someone looking for a rental. I told her you could help her find what she wants. This is Robbie; Robbie, this is... sorry, I didn't get your name.'

In her hand the coffee cup begins to crumple and Serena shakes her head. 'No, it's fine... I have to go, it's fine,' she says and leaves, coffee beginning to dribble out the side of the cup where the carboard has split.

'See what rental prices are doing to people these days,' Serena hears the woman say.

'Not my fault,' the man replies. 'Come on, Leo needs you on something.'

Serena passes a garbage bin, dumps her coffee and wipes her hand on her coat. She gets to her car in a few quick steps.

That was close, too close.

She shouldn't have gone to his workplace.

That was the agreement. That was the deal. But she wanted to see what his reaction would be and now she knows. He's angry and upset and that will make the next part so much easier.

But she should have stayed away from where he works.

*It's nearly over so what does it matter?* Serena repeats the words as she drives over to the care home for her shift.

Is it nearly over and will she get what she wants from this?

Whatever happens, there's no going back now.

Leo Palmer might be mad about his plans being cancelled but he has no idea how much worse things are going to get for him. No idea at all.

# ELEVEN

## LEO

Two Weeks Ago

Leo stares up at the ceiling of his office as he waits to leave a message with Jack who runs the smash repair business he has dealt with for years. Serena has cancelled their meeting tomorrow so he has literally nothing to look forward to this week except for the grind of daily life. The rush of anger he experienced at her cancelling surprised him. This is just fun, isn't it? He should not be this bothered. But he is bothered. He is getting used to texting her every day. He messages more than she does but she always replies immediately, as though she's waiting for him to contact her.

It's after six and Jack is obviously gone for the day. 'Yeah, Jack, mate, Leo Palmer here. Some idiot scratched up my car, every bloody panel. Give me a call so I can get it fixed. It's going to have to be an insurance job. I just wanted to check your availability and I'll get them to come out to you.' He should have made the call last week on Tuesday night or even Wednesday but he had a property go up for auction on Wednesday and a panicked client discussion on Thursday evening.

He will have to say it happened in a shopping centre parking lot, tell everyone he stopped to get lunch in between appointments.

His car told prospective clients that he was good at his job and right now he didn't feel very good at it. But every time he looked at the Porsche when it wasn't in its current damaged state, he experienced the slight thrill he felt when, after a brilliant month, he put down the deposit on the new car. Real estate ran on confidence and positivity, something that Leo has found to be in short supply lately. Serena had helped him reclaim that 'top of the world' feeling but now he didn't even have her to look forward to this week.

An email drops into his personal inbox. Mrs Denton's grandson – again. This guy is getting really annoying.

I am in Australia for the next two weeks. I think I should tell you that I have already found a lawyer. You're a lying piece of crap, Mr Palmer, and if you think I'm going to let you get away with forcing my grandmother to sell our family home, you're wrong. Watch out for me, Mr Palmer. I'm not letting you get away with this.

This is getting ridiculous. And now Peter Denton is no longer in the USA but here. That is more of a concern.

Leo had believed that the threatening emails were because he had no hope of getting over to Australia and was crossing his fingers that his threats would work. Until today.

'Shit,' mutters Leo. He may have to talk to a lawyer.

The office is quiet, with only him and Robbie still here. He has so much paperwork to get through, so much kowtowing and reassuring to do with his clients, but he just can't face any of it. He would like to sit quietly and think about Serena, just Serena and her gorgeous long hair and soft skin. Leo sighs, closes his eyes and leans back in his chair, just savouring the memory. He doesn't let himself do this often, and he shouldn't do it now, knowing that he will only see her again in nine days' time.

'It doesn't look like you're working,' he hears and he opens his eyes to see Robbie laughing at him.

'Just resting my eyes,' he says, grinning.

'You get that listing on the beaches?'

'They're still thinking about it,' Leo lies easily.

'I'm getting a burger across the road before I go over to someone to sign final papers on a rental, want to join me?'

'Sure,' says Leo, suddenly sick of sitting in his chair, of thinking about how to deal with unhappy clients.

'Will you lock up?' says Robbie.

'Yeah,' calls Leo.

He leaves the agency, looking forward to a beer and a burger. He thinks briefly about letting Diana know he won't be home for dinner but then decides not to. He's still angry with her over her reaction to the car. It wouldn't kill her to be a tad more supportive.

The bar across the road from their agency is full for a Monday night. The owner advertises a Monday night special of a burger and a beer or glass of wine for twenty dollars, a bargain for this part of town.

'Grab a table, I'll order,' says Robbie, who already knows that Leo always gets the double cheeseburger. Leo nods, knowing he should offer to pay but screw it, Robbie's not some nineteen-year-old. He can afford to treat his boss every now and again.

He finds a table right at the back, tucked away, and sits down to wait. Robbie arrives with their beers and a table number soon afterwards and sits down. The first sip of beer is magic and manages to wash away some of Leo's worries but Robbie isn't fooled.

'Something wrong?' he asks politely and Leo starts to shake

his head but then he stops, feeling the need to talk. 'I'm getting a lot of pushback,' he says.

'From?' asks Robbie after a sip of his own beer.

'The Denton woman – her grandson is threatening to get a lawyer and it's just...' Leo waves his hand, 'not my month,' and then he stops talking while a waiter puts their burgers down and collects their number.

Robbie takes a bite of his burger and chews. 'I was worried about the Denton house. You may have...' he hesitates, 'I mean it's not my place to say but maybe we should have just let her pull out of the sale.'

'She understood exactly what she was getting into. The grandson is just kicking and screaming because he's worried about his inheritance.'

'At least the father isn't in the picture. He sounds like a bit of a bastard,' says Robbie.

'It's not my problem really. I'm sure he'll turn up one day, probably at her funeral.'

'I'm sorry you're having a rough time,' says Robbie, shoving a handful of fries in his mouth. Leo looks down at his own plate where he is eating his fries slowly, not wanting to finish them. He's never had to even think about what he eats until now. Getting older was not easy. He should exercise more, especially since he's now sleeping with a twenty-eight-year-old.

'Yeah well, it'll come right, it usually does,' says Leo, even though he doesn't believe the words.

'Look, it's over now. Hopefully the guy just backs off. And sales will pick up. You're a good guy and it'll turn around.'

Leo takes a sip of his beer, gazes out at the crowd, all laughing and talking, and notices that he's probably the oldest guy in the place, not something he likes to notice.

'Sometimes I don't feel like a good guy,' says Leo.

'Why?' asks Robbie.

Leo takes another bite of his burger, regretting his words. Where did that come from and why had he said it out loud?

'Just... I'm just... having a bad month,' he says.

'Leo, everyone has those. You're a good guy. You take care of your family and you don't cheat on your wife or hit your kids. Stuff like that makes you a bad person, not pushing a little to get the job done.'

'I've been married for nearly fourteen years,' says Leo. 'Marriage is hard.'

Robbie finishes his last bite of burger, chews while he studies Leo. 'Are you telling me something?' he asks and for a moment, Leo considers a confession, wonders what it would feel like to tell someone else about Serena, about how beautiful she is, how amazing. It would feel like a win. He can imagine Robbie's admiring gaze as he explains that he's sleeping with a twenty-eight-year-old woman.

But just as quickly as he has this thought he squashes it down. Keeping up a double life is hard enough without anyone else knowing. And Robbie probably wouldn't understand his cheating. He's met Diana and likes her, even told Leo he was 'punching above his weight' with his wife, meaning that he had married a woman better than he deserved. And Robbie is in that phase of his life where he is looking for something more permanent, moaning every Monday about bad Tinder dates and the exhaustion of making conversation with someone new every week. Robbie wouldn't understand how stifling marriage is – he thinks it's the rosy future.

'Nah, just saying. You'll find out soon enough.'

'Ha, I wish,' smiles Robbie. 'Want another beer?'

'Maybe,' says Leo as he thinks about how late he will be home tonight. It's not like Diana will miss him anyway. She's probably watching something on television, immersed in one of her streaming platforms, her eyes glazed over.

'Your shout if you do,' says Robbie and then his buzzing phone distracts him and he holds up a finger so he can answer.

'What?' he says. 'No... no, don't sweat it, Leo and I are across the road; we'll get there now.'

Robbie hangs up. 'Someone's trashed the office,' he says, his face pale in the yellow light from the bar. 'The police are there, and they've been trying to contact someone from the agency but no one's picking up. They got hold of Martin but he's still in the Blue Mountains and only coming back tomorrow. That was him.'

Leo pulls his phone out of his pocket to find a host of missed calls from a number he doesn't recognise and three missed calls from Martin Gantry, head of the Gantry Real Estate Agency, as well. He put his phone on silent just before dinner.

The two men hurry across the road to their office building where the whole place is lit up. Outside, a police car sits in the street, red and blue lights swinging in slow circles.

Inside, Robbie and Leo are asked for their driver's licences by a young policewoman with a gun strapped to her leg.

'What happened?' asked Leo.

The policewoman points to the bar. 'Someone waiting outside saw a person smashing things up in here, called us in. Where have you been?'

'We were across the road, having a burger; we were inside,' says Robbie.

'The damage seems to be confined to one office,' she says. 'Please don't touch anything until we've had a proper look.'

'I just want to check out my office,' says Leo.

A creeping sense of dread alerts him to what he's going to see and a sinking sensation fills his chest when his suspicion is proved correct.

The only trashed office is his.

The desktop has been thrown on the floor, paper files

strewn everywhere, the vase that held the flowers that are replaced every week smashed and leaking onto the carpet.

His desk is covered in pieces of A4 paper with the word 'Liar' in thick black marker on each one.

**LIAR LIAR LIAR LIAR LIAR**

He can taste the beer and the burger in his mouth, his stomach twisting and bloated.

Leo knows who this is. He knows who has done this.

'Geez, mate,' says Robbie, coming to stand next to him and survey the damage, 'you don't think this is...?'

'Shut it,' hisses Leo, not wanting to talk about Mrs Denton's grandson and his threats to the police.

'Perhaps you could give us a list of people who may have something against you, Mr Palmer,' says the young policewoman.

'There's no one,' lies Leo. 'This is just random. I don't want to do anything except clean up.'

'We have to take statements and dust for prints,' says the policewoman. 'You can't clean up until we've done that. Do you know how to access the security camera footage?' she asks, pointing to the cameras in the corners of the office.

'Leo?' asks Robbie. 'I haven't been here long enough to know.'

Leo nods, a headache tightening around his head like a band. 'The cameras are linked to Martin's phone but they're also linked to the reception computer.' The policewoman nods and then stands over Leo's shoulder as he sits down at Blake's desk and switches on the computer, quickly accessing the security footage. The office in darkness comes up, only filtered light from the window that is always kept lit, so the pictures of homes are always easy to see, and the streetlights outside provide any light.

A shadowy figure, dressed all in black including a black ski mask, seems to move through and then Leo switches the camera to his office where the destruction is taking place. The policeman peers at the footage, but the man, Leo assumes it's a man from the build, is completely in black, right down to gloves. It takes only minutes before the office is wrecked and the man lifts his top slightly and pulls out a sheaf of paper, scattering the A4 pages over Leo's desk.

And then he looks directly at the camera and points to himself and then points at the camera. The message is obvious to Leo. *I'm coming for you.* His headache intensifies, his heart thumping in his chest.

'Mr Palmer, are you certain there is no one who might have an issue with you?' the policewoman asks, her tone coated in scepticism.

Leo debates saying something for a moment – just a moment – but just like with his car, he has an inkling that getting the police involved would actually cause him more harm than good. They would interview Mrs Denton; they would interview the grandson. Real estate runs on reputation and this is just the kind of thing that would find its way onto news sites once the police are involved. He has to protect his career.

'No, no one,' he says, standing and walking away from the computer.

'I'll need that footage,' says the policewoman but Leo keeps moving, away from her and back to his office where Robbie is surveying the damage as a second police officer, a man, takes photographs.

'You can go, Robbie, I'll sort this,' he says firmly.

'I'll help you clean up,' says Robbie.

'Thanks, thanks, Robbie,' says Leo, his voice tight. 'Sorry about...' He stops speaking as the policeman moves close to him, photographing the smashed vase.

The policewoman comes up behind him. 'There's no forced

entry,' she says.

'You locked up, didn't you?' asks Robbie.

Leo looks around his office and then feels in his pocket for his keys. Had he locked up? He thought he had but when he tries to remember, he can't actually see himself putting his key into the lock.

'I did,' he says, conscious that if his computer is broken, insurance will pay for a new one, but not if he didn't lock up. He needs some time to think about it, needs everyone gone so he can just think.

'You might as well go, Robbie. I'll stay and wait for this to be done.' He wants Robbie and his suspicions about who might have done this out of here.

'You sure you don't want me to stay? I can push back the signing of the rental agreement.'

'Nah, go ahead.'

Robbie nods and turns to go. 'Leo,' he says, 'what were you going to say in the bar when you told me marriage was hard? I feel like you actually wanted to say something else.' *Marriage is hard, having kids is hard, having bills is hard, having nothing to look forward to is the hardest of all. Having your office trashed is hard. Being threatened is hard. All this shit is hard.*

'Nothing, just that,' says Leo, 'just that.'

'If you could wait over there, sir,' says the policewoman and Leo takes a seat on the black leather sofa where clients usually wait.

He can feel the long night ahead of him and the long week to come. If he had Serena to look forward to tomorrow, everything would have been better and even this little hiccup wouldn't have bothered him.

Leo drops his head into his hands.

Is it Mrs Denton's son or grandson who trashed his office or someone else entirely? Unbidden, a thought occurs and he pictures his desk drawer at home, the one crammed with letters, but he immediately dismisses the idea. He would know if he had anything to worry about.

'If you could just come in and do an inventory for us so we can see if anything has been taken, please, sir,' says the young policewoman. She has brown hair tied back and dark eyes and Leo knows, as he looks around his office, that she does not believe him when he says that no one has anything against him.

'It's an odd thing to do, isn't it, sir?' she says.

'What's an odd thing to do?'

'Leave the word "liar" on a whole lot of pieces of paper. Are you married?'

Leo feels his stomach churn and sweat beads on his forehead. 'I am.' He hadn't even considered that this might be to do with Serena. But of course, it fits. The 'boyfriend' she says doesn't exist could very well have done this to his office, especially if he also damaged Leo's car.

'And your wife is...'

'At home with our sons. There's nothing missing that I can see and I'm exhausted. So if you're done with me, I really would like to go home.'

'Of course,' she says, a small lift at the side of her mouth infuriating him. 'We'll be done soon.'

Leo returns to the sofa and takes out his phone, scrolling down to Serena's last message, which he did not delete.

His hand hovers over it as he wonders if she would somehow make him feel better about this but, after a moment, he just deletes the message. He doesn't want to believe it's some jealous boyfriend, because that would mean never seeing her again. His mind circles back to Peter Denton and his ex-con father. That makes more sense. What he can't tell the police is that the list of people who might have an issue with him is growing by the day, and has been for a long time.

He closes his eyes as he waits.

Next Tuesday can't come soon enough.

# TWELVE

## DIANA

One Week Ago

In the coffee shop near her clinic, Diana is waiting for a woman. She knows she will be younger than her. She imagines that she will have smooth skin, a flat stomach, a perfect smile. She will look like Diana did before time and children.

Diana is waiting for perfection. Leo would have chosen perfection. But there must be something else as well. As far as she can tell, and she has been searching the past four years for clues, Leo has never done more than sleep with someone at a conference. She has no idea if it's been the same woman or different women. But she doesn't think it has been happening in Sydney. She believes she would have noticed. She would have, wouldn't she? The days have passed so slowly as she waited for this meeting, she thought she might go mad. But she has taken the time to really study Leo, to observe him, searching for clues that he is in love with someone else. But either this woman is lying or Leo is the consummate liar, adept at being two separate people every single day of his life. He is worried about work, a little short tempered with the boys but nothing that would point to him being in love with or even just involved with someone else. And yet, she is here to meet his mistress.

And because she knows he is capable of this; she is constantly drawn back to the office and the letters. What else is he capable of? He wouldn't even know if she took one out of the pile to look at, but somehow, she is not able to do it. What do the letters say and does she want to know? Why would this particular prisoner be writing to Leo? It's too much. There are too many Leo secrets swirling around her. She needs to deal with this first and then she will deal with the letters. She closes her eyes and tries to picture her again, to prepare herself for the woman Leo would have chosen.

The worst thing about being cheated on is the humiliation of living with someone who believes you are too stupid or oblivious to know what they are doing.

Being too stupid to know about conferences was one thing – they happened in hotels and usually interstate. Being too stupid to know about an actual affair happening right where Leo lived with his family was something else entirely. How on earth will she be able to trust her judgement if this is an affair and not just a hook-up?

She has ordered a coffee but it's growing cold in its paper cup. Lying next to her husband in bed last night, Diana had tried to channel calm and control so that she could use the situation to her advantage.

Leo had come in late and she had simply pretended to be asleep. He left early this morning as well without even talking to her. Was he with this woman? Is that where he was last night?

As the night hours passed, she had tried not to allow the happy memories, and there were so many, to derail her from the track she was on.

But her mind had taken her back to her honeymoon in London and Leo laughing at how excited she was to see the

Tower of London. He had insisted on buying her every kitschy souvenir and she still has them all in a box; a small British flag, a mug painted with a beautiful portrait of the late Princess Diana's face, a plate with a picture of Buckingham Palace, a T-shirt with Big Ben. She would be embarrassed to show anyone but it had meant so much to her at the time that he loved buying them for her.

The Sunday morning she found out she was pregnant and the look on his face when he came downstairs and the test was lying on the table next to his coffee cup. His tears when they found out they were having twins and the way he held her hand during labour, whispering, 'You've got this, I love you, you've got this.' She couldn't help her tears as the memories rose within her and she was back on the seesaw. Could they save their marriage? If she confronts him and demands he go to therapy, would he agree to do it? Does she want to do it? If she had confronted him a few years ago – would they be here now? Is this somehow her fault for not letting him know what she suspected?

Finally, her brain simply played their wedding song, 'You're Beautiful', on a continuous loop until she fell asleep.

And now she is here, waiting to meet the woman who means the end of her marriage.

Diana looks around but there's no one who fits the bill. She takes out her phone, checks that she has the right time. She's ten minutes late. Maybe this is all a colossal joke?

A man walks towards her and stops at her table.

'Diana,' he says.

She doesn't register that he's used her name at first.

'I only need one chair,' she says, assuming he wants the third chair at the table for himself.

'Diana,' he says again and something cold slithers through her veins as she looks at him properly. He's a large man, his face not unattractive but his looks hampered by a crooked nose.

Who is this? Who is this person who has her number? What has she gotten herself into? She sits up straight, glances at the café door. How fast can she run?

'I'm here to meet you,' he says softly, his stance wide, fists clenched by his side.

Diana's breath catches in her throat and she coughs, pushes her chair back and stands.

'What is this?' she says.

'You need to sit down so I can explain some things,' he says firmly.

'No way, this is... what exactly are you playing at?' she demands, her voice rising and catching the attention of other people in the coffee shop.

'I need to talk to you about your husband, Leo.' He raises his fists slightly and then seems to catch himself, lowering his hands and letting them relax.

Without her permission, Diana's body drops back into the chair. She is stunned. Leo is having an affair with a man?

'I don't...' she says and he waves his hands.

'I'm not the one sleeping with him. I'm here to represent her.' He drops into a chair opposite her and waits, his stare disconcerting.

'Why? What do you want? What do both of you want?' Fear prickles along her skin. This is not just a one-off at a conference; this is not even an ongoing affair. This is more than that.

'You need to hear this story. You need to listen,' he says.

'No, you need to listen. I don't know what this is but Leo is the father of my children. I have ten-year-old boys named Rowan and Sawyer; see?' She picks up her phone and turns it around to show the man a picture of herself and her boys, all three of them on the beach crouched around a sandcastle, the wind in their hair. The boys are looking up at the camera, glee on their faces, and she is laughing because Leo just told a terrible dad joke so they would all smile. 'This is a family, so before you speak you need to know that this is my family and I will do everything I can to protect them.' She realises that she has bared her teeth. She will do anything she can to protect them, she will.

The man doesn't even look at the photo. 'You're not the only one with a family so you need to keep quiet and let me talk.' His voice catches on the word family, as though he might actually cry but then he looks at her, holding her with his direct stare.

Diana wants her legs to move, wants to get up out of the chair and leave. She will go to Leo immediately, and they will go to the police. This is some kind of scam or something. But the man is big, scary-looking. Her body won't respond.

'Let me start at the beginning,' he says.

Diana folds her arms. She will go from here to Leo and the police but she listens carefully because then she can tell the police everything they need to know.

The man begins to speak, his voice low so that others in the café can't hear, some anguish in his blue eyes, his hands clenching and unclenching.

Diana listens, her horror growing. And she realises there is so much more to this than an affair, so much more than some of Leo's questionable behaviour at work, and she has had no idea about any of it.

She has no idea who her husband is. No idea at all.

# THIRTEEN
## SERENA

One Week Ago

In the restaurant bathroom, Serena smooths on light gloss over her red lips as she stares into the mirror. Today she ends it. Lunch has only been ordinary today. Leo insisted they choose a different hotel after his car got damaged at the last one so of course she had to agree.

*Just checking that we're still good for today*, he texted her this morning.

*Why wouldn't we be?*

**Well, last week something came up with work. I know work comes first so I just wanted to make sure.**

Serena never knew that someone could sound so petulant and sulky over text but Leo managed it.

*I can't wait to see you.*

*Me too xxx*

Today they are in another anonymous hotel in the city but one with a slightly less salubrious air. Things feel tired and old and the restaurant served up a fairly poor example of a risotto with slightly chewy rice and an overabundance of cheese.

There is a churning in her stomach which may be the oil and garlic or it may be what she's about to do.

'Come on,' she whispers to herself in the mirror, 'you can do this.' She nods and then leaves the bathroom to find Leo having an argument with the waiter.

'There's no way it's cancelled,' he says, his face slightly red with frustration and humiliation as he holds his credit card. 'It's my bloody card. I would know if it was cancelled.' Serena can see that he wants to be yelling but the situation is not one in which people yell.

'I'm so sorry, sir,' mumbles the waiter who is a young man with a prominent Adam's apple, obviously unused to anyone getting angry with him in the nice, quiet hotel. The restaurant is mostly filled with elderly diners.

'It's okay, I've got it,' she says, opening her phone to her credit card, more to save the waiter any more strife than to save Leo any humiliation. His face is red to the tips of his ears.

His day is about to get a lot worse than just a credit card that won't work.

'No, it's fine,' says Leo, holding up his hand to stop her. 'I can use another card.' He fishes through his wallet and finds another card, a personal card because he has a separate one for business lunches, and Serena is a business lunch – she's in real estate, after all.

'I don't mind,' she tries but Leo shakes his head.

Serena nods and walks away from him towards the door of the restaurant, knowing that he would prefer her not to witness his embarrassment but enjoying it all the same.

She wanders into the lobby and studies an oversized painting consisting of a jumble of colours. 'I have no idea what that was about,' says Leo, coming up behind her. 'I've truly had the month from hell and now I have to go back to the book-keeper and sort this out.'

'Poor baby,' she says, resting her hand lightly on his arm and he smiles, his whole body relaxing.

Upstairs in the room, she cannot find a way to relax enough and he notices it. She stares past his shoulder, willing him to be done.

'Something wrong?' he asks when it's over.

'I've been thinking,' she says.

'Mm?' he says, running his fingers across her belly. 'Tell me what you've been thinking.'

'I've been thinking that we've had a lot of fun but maybe we're done now,' she says, moving away from him and wrapping her body in the sheet.

Leo laughs.

Serena watches him, silent, waits for him to get it.

'Wait, you're serious?'

'Leo, this was only ever for a short time, you knew that.' She sits up straight, holding the sheet tighter against her body. Anxiety is thrumming through her as she waits for his reaction, unsure exactly what he will do.

'No... it's only been a few weeks, and we're so good together. You know that. We have a great time. Why do you want to mess with that? It's so good.' He rubs his hands through his hair as he talks, his face colouring again. Humiliation is humiliation whether your credit card is refused or a woman dumps you.

'Leo,' she says softly, leaning forward to touch him on the arm, 'it's not like you're going to leave your wife for me, is it?'

'No,' he says, standing. 'I mean obviously, but you never said you wanted that. Do you want that?' He runs his hands through his hair again, a desperate sadness on his face.

'Not at all,' she says firmly, looking away from his naked body, not wanting to see it now that she'll never have to look at it again.

'Then why? Why are you doing this? We can keep going as we are. We can just...' He throws up his hands. 'Why?' he asks again. He looks around the room for his clothes and begins getting dressed.

She waits while he pulls on his pants. 'Why?' he asks again. Serena clutches the sheet more tightly around her, wishing she were in the hot shower washing this away. She had imagined that his ego would make him go quietly, even that he would agree, to save himself the humiliation of being dumped.

'Because it's done,' she says. 'It's just done.' She clenches the muscles in her jaw, keeping her voice firm. And then she stands up and takes a few steps towards the bathroom. She can dart in there and lock the door if this gets out of control.

Leo shakes his head. 'Was this just a game to you?'

She listens for a threat but he mostly sounds sad and so she relaxes.

'It was a game to both of us, wasn't it?' she says softly. 'This is not real life, Leo, and you know it. You didn't think it would just go on until you were bored, did you? At home you have a wife and kids and you just stick them in a box and come here and pretend they don't exist. What is that if not a game? You're playing a game of pretend and so was I but I'm done now. I have to get back to work and get on with my life.'

'I can't believe you're doing this,' he says, some anger creeping in. 'And what life do you have to get on with? You said there was no one else in your life.'

'What does it matter if there is, Leo? This has always just been a side thing. I know barely anything about you. You're hiding so much of yourself.'

'I'm not hiding anything.'

'Oh Leo,' she says, 'we're all hiding something.'

'Tell me what you want to know, anything... just tell me.'

Should she push this now while he is here and vulnerable? *No, not now. Not yet.*

'Listen, I don't think you wanted more than this. You just want to be the one to decide it's over. But I've made the decision for us.' Her fingers are beginning to cramp because she's holding the sheet so tightly.

Leo stares at her as he slowly pulls on his shirt. 'I don't believe you want this to end. Is this a ploy to get me to confess my love for you or tell you I'll leave my wife or something?' He's nearly fully dressed now and she's pleased about that. He will leave soon. Will he leave soon?

'Well, believe it,' says Serena, irritated. 'It's not a ploy and please don't use the word "love". Trust comes before love and there's no trust between us. We barely know each other. It's over.' She moves to the bathroom door before this can escalate any further. 'Please leave while I shower,' she says.

He moves across the room to her, grabs her arm. 'What if I'm not done talking?' he spits. He is holding on tightly, causing her pain, but worse than the pain is the panic that spreads through her. She had not imagined he was capable of this but now that she is here, she wonders at her own stupidity. Obviously, he is capable of this. He is capable of a lot worse. Her need to keep herself safe fires up inside her and the panic is drowned by a flash of anger, mostly at herself for not handling this better.

'Let me go,' she growls, and Leo lets go and steps back.

'Sorry, I just, you can't just make this decision. We're... you don't understand, you're the only thing in my life that I look forward to. Please let's just meet one more time and then we can see how we feel.'

Serena steps into the bathroom, pulling the sheet with her, grateful that her bag with her clothes is already in there. 'That's so sad. You have a wife and children at home and you should be thankful for them every day but you're not, you're here with me chasing some high and that's fine but I'm done now. Go back to your life.' She turns and pulls the sheet to her feet so it won't get caught when she closes the door.

'What do you know about my life, Serena?' he hisses.

'Nothing,' she says. *So much more than you would believe.*

'You've really just been playing with me, haven't you?' he sneers.

Serena hears the escalation in his tone, feels his anger coming off him. He doesn't like this at all.

'I'm done talking, Leo. Don't make me ask again. Just leave.'

'Bitch,' he mutters.

'Really?' she asks.

'I'm not a goddamn toy, Serena. You can't just use men like they're playthings. How many men have you done this with? Are you some kind of whore? Is it just about the nice lunches and the fancy hotel? Are you even in real estate or do you just trawl the conferences waiting to pick up some idiot?' He steps away from her and grabs his tie from an armchair, throwing it around his neck.

'Careful, Leo, be careful of what you say. This was fun. We had a good time but now it's over,' she says, keeping her tone firm, even with her heart dancing in her chest. 'Don't be here when I get out,' she instructs him.

He starts to move towards her again, but she steps back, shuts the bathroom door, locks it.

She pulls her phone out of her bag and holds it in her hand. If he starts pounding on the door, she knows what to do. Her whole body is trembling. Should she get dressed? Should she wait? Should she send a message now?

Sitting on the edge of the too-small bathtub, she listens for his movements in the room, waiting for the door to slam.

But when she doesn't hear it, she sends a text.

*I've ended it. He won't leave the hotel room.*

**I told you this was a bad idea. And you've got
nothing from him.**

*I'm still not done. Just get him out of here.*

Serena starts the shower but doesn't get in, instead pushing
her ear up against the bathroom door, straining to hear over the
rushing water.

Relief floods her body when she hears Leo's phone ring.

'Diana, I can't talk now,' she hears and then, 'Yes, right, fine.
Look, I have to go, work is calling me.'

'Hello, hey, Blake, yes... no, I can't deal with that... okay,
fine, fine, I'm coming. Shit,' Leo mutters and then there is a
rustle of movement and then the beautiful sound of a door slamming hard, fury in the force of it.

Serena covers the wig and steps into the shower and washes
away everything she has done over the past few weeks, luxuri-
ating in the hot water even as she worries that when she opens
the door he will still be there.

By the time she is dressed in her clothes and has removed
her make-up and the wig properly, half an hour has passed.

Opening the door slowly, she holds her breath. But he's
gone.

Time to move on.

She only feels completely safe once she's in her car on the
way home and, even then, she keeps looking in her rear-view
mirror, waiting to see his car appear.

But Leo has gone back to work or back home. She has done
what needed to be done.

And Leo has no idea what's coming now.

# FOURTEEN

## LEO

One Week Ago

Leo taps his foot impatiently, waiting for the valet to bring his car around. He paid extra for the valet parking, hoping to avoid a repeat of the last time he was in a hotel parking lot.

'*Bitch, bitch, bitch,*' he mutters as he waits. His fury is so intense, it's making him sweat despite the frigid wind tunnel of a garage. She just used him and now she's done. Women shouldn't be allowed to get away with that kind of behaviour. Should he text her? Maybe he should text her and just ask if they can meet for a drink to talk, just to talk. He can convince her to keep meeting, he's sure of it.

He looks down at his phone and, on impulse, calls her number as he stares out at the parking lot.

'The number you have dialled is disconnected. Please check the number before calling again.'

Leo shakes his head. He's not concentrating, obviously. He closes down everything on his phone and takes a deep breath, opening it again and finding the contact he's saved her number under. What will he say? He hopes his brain catches up by the time she answers.

'The number you have dialled is disconnected. Please check the number before calling again.'

The valet pulls up with his car as Leo stares down at his phone. How is this possible?

'Um, you may want to get your car checked out, there's a weird smell,' says the young man who had gone to find his car, and Leo looks up from his phone, realising that the man is holding his keys for him.

'What do you mean? There wasn't a smell when I arrived here.'

The man who is bald with a black beard shrugs his shoulders. 'I don't know. I only started my shift half an hour ago.'

Leo opens the car door and immediately gags. The car stinks of something rotting, something dead. The smell is acrid and sharp, immediately catching the back of his throat.

'What the... Someone has put something in my car. Did you look for it?' he yells.

'I don't—' says the man.

'Look for it,' shouts Leo, 'it must be somewhere.' He opens all the doors of the car and searches under the seats and then he pops the boot and looks there. He can find nothing. Frustrated, he opens the bonnet and looks in there as well. The smell seems stronger around the engine. Using his phone as a torch, Leo squints at the engine, trying to figure out if anything has been moved or is out of place. He can see nothing. The man is not helping him at all, just watching him, and Leo wants to wring his neck. He closes all the car doors and gets on his knees, peering under the car.

'I have to go and get another car now,' the man says and Leo stands and turns to find the man standing with an elderly couple, white haired and bent, holding hands. They are staring at him and Leo can see he looks like a lunatic.

'This is unacceptable,' he says. 'This happened in your garage.'

The man regards him quietly. 'I'm sorry, sir, but I'm just here to park the cars,' he says politely, too politely, and Leo hears the threat of something behind the words. The man is bigger than Leo, his muscles bulging in the stupid maroon waistcoat the hotel obviously makes him wear. But he's not the kind of person Leo should start with.

'We do need to get to a doctor's appointment,' the old man says and Leo loses the will to keep going.

His shoulders sag. He doesn't have the energy for this. He climbs into the driver's seat and opens all the windows, letting the cold air from the garage blow through the car.

He drives off with a screech of his tyres, hating every single hotel parking lot in the city, hating his life, hating Serena and hating, with furious rage, the valet who didn't care about Leo's anger.

This cannot be a coincidence. Serena must have a boyfriend, someone who's pissed that she's cheating. She should have told him that she was attached. That's why she didn't answer him when he asked if she'd been lying about a boyfriend. There's obviously a boyfriend, and he feels like a right idiot for believing her when she said there wasn't. Obviously, he hasn't exactly been thinking with his brain over the last few weeks. But if there is a boyfriend, why cheat? *You have a wife, why are you cheating?* 'That's different,' says Leo aloud, silencing the thought.

As the wind hits his face, slicing against his cheeks, it occurs to him that maybe that's how Serena gets her kicks. Maybe this is just entertainment. She and the boyfriend set up unsuspecting men and then mess with their cars. Why? What do they gain?

Scenarios run through his head. Serena and the boyfriend are a detective couple hired by Diana to trap him into cheating;

Serena and the boyfriend are a couple of psychos who just enjoy this; Serena and her boyfriend are... He exhausts himself with possibilities.

When he gets back to the office, he's in no mood to talk to anyone. He leaves the windows open to air out the car. Next week it's going in to get fixed and the smash repairers will have to look for the smell as well. He doesn't have time for this shit now.

Robbie is waiting for him outside his office. 'Peter Denton sent an email to the whole agency,' he starts but before Robbie can finish telling him the latest development in his shitty life, Leo holds up his hand. 'I just don't give a damn. I'll deal with it later. I need to do some work,' he says and he goes into his office, even as Robbie's confused stare follows him. He shuts the door and sinks into his chair behind his desk.

On impulse he googles Serena's name, wanting to see if anything new has been added. Maybe the LinkedIn profile is fake and she's an entirely different person.

But there's nothing on her. Even the LinkedIn profile is gone.

Leo tries different searches, his tapping growing more frenetic as he fails to locate the woman he's been sleeping with for the past five weeks.

He finds a Serena Burns who lives in Queensland and has red hair, and Serena Burns who is in business development and looks to be at least sixty, and Serena Burns who is an artist with flowing blonde hair, and a whole host of other Serena Burnses. But no matter how he enters her name, Serena Burns real estate, Serena Burns commercial real estate, Serena Burns commercial, and anything else he can think of, she's not there.

"Serena Burns detective", he types, but that yields nothing at all. He searches Instagram and Facebook and even TikTok but he cannot find her.

And finally, he takes his hands off the computer and pushes

his chair away from his desk. He leans back, a sick realisation flooding through him.

He's been scammed. He knows that for sure now. He's just not certain if the woman, whoever she is, has had her fun and it's over. Or if there is worse to come.

His company credit card was declined today. Has she stolen money from him? They have limits on their cards and when they reach those limits they stop working. Had he fallen asleep after sex and she copied his card? He needs to go through all the transactions.

He goes to look up his account but he can't log on. He keeps typing in his usual login details before he remembers that details are routinely changed for security. He'll need to ask Blake, the receptionist, who keeps all that information, to do it for him. He can't be bothered with it right now.

He folds his arms on his desk and drops his head down, like he used to do when school just got too much for him. He is flooded with a feeling he hates: shame. He is ashamed of himself for being so stupid. At least he never told Robbie about her. How could he have been such a prize idiot? He's too old to be making mistakes like this.

A memory surfaces from when Leo was only four, a memory involving his father. His father looked like he does – still looks like him with a full head of grey hair and the same green eyes – but his father was an old-style kind of parent, nothing like Leo is with his boys. *When are you with your boys?* Leo dismisses the thought. He may not be that involved but at least he doesn't hit, hurt and sneer at his kids. He's not a terrible dad. He's not the best kind of father but he's not terrible either. Maybe Diana would disagree with that. But his father raised him with a subtle cruelty that sank in and torments Leo even now, forcing him to question himself constantly but to never admit that to anyone. Every failed sale makes him think of his father, every defeat is accompanied by a vision of the old man shaking his head in disappointment. Leo never was and never will be good enough for his father.

He remembers being four years old with his head caught in the balustrade of the stairwell.

He has no idea why he stuck his head in between the two timber posts, probably to impress his two-year-old sister, Emily, who had been watching him with wide eyes, drool on her chin. 'Watch me, Em, watch me,' he remembers saying. His head went through fine but then he was stuck.

His mother was out, at the grocery store or something, and only his father was home.

'Help, help, help,' Leo remembers screaming as he pulled his head, bruising his ears in his attempt to escape.

And then his father appeared, the newspaper he had been reading still in his hand. 'What on earth are you doing, Leo?'

'I'm stuck, stuck,' he had cried, tears dripping onto the navy-blue carpet below the stairs.

'Why did you do that? What a stupid thing to do.'

'Daddy, I'm stuck,' Leo shouted, believing that all he needed to do was make his father understand and his father would help him, would free him.

'I can see you're stuck. But you got yourself into this, Leo, and if you're going to do idiotic things, you should know how to get yourself out of them. It'll be a good lesson.' And then he had just walked away. Emily had tried ineffectually to help by pulling him from his shoulders until he shouted at her to stop and then she had wandered off to do something else.

The timber on the stairwell was strong and no matter what Leo did, he couldn't get free and the more he tried, the harder it got as his ears swelled from being hit against the balustrade. Finally, he gave up and sat still, crouched on his knees on the stairs, his neck aching with the strange angle, and waited until his mother came home to rescue him. She yelled at his father for not helping as she rubbed oil on his ears and moved his head in a way that finally freed him. His father only laughed, 'He won't do that again, will he.'

*Why are you so stupid, Leo? How could you get yourself into something like* this? Leo hears the phrases in his father's voice.

Is this whole thing over now? Are Serena and her psycho boyfriend done with him?

Or is something else coming?

He doesn't think he can cope with one more thing. Not one more thing.

The email from Peter Denton crosses his mind but he cannot deal with it. How much worse can this day get? How much worse can his life get? If this is some kind of weird karma for something he's done in the past, if it is, surely it's over now.

Leo keeps his head on his desk, closing his eyes.

He wills the day to be over so he can start again, so he can fix his mistakes and do better. That's all he needs to do, start again.

# FIFTEEN

## DIANA

One Week Ago

'And then I got ten out of ten and Rowan got so angry that he punched me on the arm,' says Sawyer. He is talking about the spelling test he and his brother took in class today and it reminds Diana that she needs to ask about separating the boys in school next year.

'You shouldn't have done that, Rowan,' says Diana as she stops the car at a traffic light but she's sure that the boys can hear she's not really present, not really concerned about their day at school. After the meeting at the café, she had struggled to listen to the mothers at the clinic, admonished herself to 'pay attention', each time she had to ask a question again. Fortunately, the patients from the afternoon were all just there for general checks and were all done quite quickly.

Behind her a car hoots.

'It's green, it's green,' shouts Rowan.

'Stop shouting at her,' says Sawyer.

'Shut up,' says Rowan.

'Both of you, stop,' says Diana.

She doesn't know how to stop her thoughts as they whirl in her head. She didn't want to believe anything the man said and she certainly didn't want to participate in the scheme he and the woman have going.

At home, she makes the boys a snack, her hands moving automatically as she cuts up fruit and vegetables.

'I hate strawberries,' whines Rowan.

'I love them,' says Sawyer.

'Eat it or leave it, I don't care,' says Diana and she leaves them in the kitchen, making her way to Leo's office.

Inside, she shuts the door and locks it.

She opens the drawer of the filing cabinet, terrified that Leo will have moved the key, but hopeful as well. She doesn't want to know.

But the key is still there. Leo would never suspect her of going through his stuff without his permission. It's not the kind of person Diana is. But after today, she has no idea what kind of a person she is and she certainly has no idea who Leo is.

She opens the drawer, pulling slightly and then using her hand to push down the letters so she can pull it all the way out.

She starts with the one on the bottom, opening it as carefully as she can. It rips a little anyway but she doesn't care.

And then she sits back on her haunches and begins to read.

*Dear Leo,*

*I'm begging you...*

# SIXTEEN

## SERENA

Three Days Ago

It takes her a few shots to get the photo just right, to make sure that the red flush of humiliation is not obvious on her breasts and to make sure that the tattoo on the side of her chest is visible. The tattoo he thinks is a heart but it's hard to see what it really is because of the twisting tendrils and tiny flowers.

Studying the picture she shakes her head, wishing she didn't have to do this. She's never done something like this before and she had never imagined that she ever would. But this is her last chance to end this without anyone getting hurt.

This is the final part of the plan, the part she hoped wouldn't be necessary, but it's nothing compared to what will happen if it doesn't work.

And she reasons that she's not sending the picture to him, not giving him a permanent reminder of her body. She's sending the picture to his wife, who's a nurse. And she's not sending anything but the picture, her face chopped off by the top of the frame.

When she's satisfied, she quickly dresses again, shivering in the cool air.

Serena Burns would probably think nothing of sending a picture of her breasts to a man or a woman and she tries to find a level of Serena Burns's confidence and attitude of not caring inside her as she keys in the mobile number.

Taking a deep breath, she attaches the photo and hits send.

And then she needs to get out of her apartment, to do something in the cold winter wind so that all of this disappears as her body attempts to stay warm. She will walk to the coffee shop and buy herself a hot chocolate and ask for extra marshmallows, the way she did when she was a child. The way she would when her mother came home early from work and took her on a special girls' afternoon out. The feeling of doing something despicable or doing something she is ethically against is bitter in her mouth. She walks fast, her body heating up quickly under her puffer coat.

At the coffee shop, she orders and then she sits at a table and gazes out at the sidewalk where people are moving back and forth, parcels in their hands, or on their phones, some laughing, some in intense conversations.

She has an hour before her shift starts.

She keeps checking her phone but she's not sure what she expects from Leo Palmer's wife.

The hot chocolate is overly sweet but she drinks it anyway. There's nothing she can do now except wait. She'll know when his wife has shown him the picture.

And that will happen soon enough.

As she stands up to leave a text comes in and she glances at it quickly.

*I'm still not sure about this.*

*Trust me when I tell you: you have no choice,* Serena replies.

She leaves the café.

Leo's wife knows some of the story. But she doesn't know everything. And it's the things she doesn't know about that could lead to her and her family getting hurt. That's exactly what Serena is trying to avoid. No one needs to get hurt except the one person who deserves it. No one needs to get hurt except Leo Palmer.

# SEVENTEEN

## LEO

Three Days Ago

Pulling into the driveway, Leo feels exhaustion descend.

He's been holding it together for days but it's so wearying. Everything that has happened piles up and he wishes there was a way to wipe his mind for just a bit.

Serena was the one bright spot in his week, the one good thing, and now that's done.

The next conference isn't until next year and that feels like a long time away but even if it was tomorrow, he wouldn't be able to find someone else to soothe his soul. *Come on, mate. It's not like you loved her.* But maybe, just maybe, he did?

The light is on in the living room and he watches Diana pass by the window, a loaded laundry basket in her arms. It's after 7 p.m. and she must be tired from work as well, tired from seeing her patients and from dealing with the boys. He knows she will have cooked dinner for them and is now embarking on an endless list of chores that repeat every week. It seems to be enough for her. Why isn't this enough for him? Their marriage is strained at the moment but maybe it can be rescued. She has suggested going to therapy and the idea made him wince but maybe she has a point. Maybe he should concentrate on finding happiness with what he has. It's more than some people have. More than a lot of people have.

He shivers in the car because all the windows are open and once the heater is off the winter chill grabs hold quickly. The smell goes away with the windows open but returns as soon as he closes them. Only three more days until the car goes in for repair. He pulls into the garage and gets out of the car, leaving the windows open and hoping, praying, that the smell is gone in the morning. He's not even going to discuss it with Diana.

He'll go in and have dinner, watch some television and then go to bed. Tomorrow will be another day.

He grabs his briefcase and gets out of the car, moving quickly to get inside where the house is warmed by the gas fireplace.

In the kitchen, he pours himself a generous glass of red wine from the bottle on the counter that Diana has opened and sniffs the air appreciatively. Roast chicken.

'Dinner, boys,' he hears Diana call and then she comes into the kitchen. She's still in her work uniform of black pants and a matching black top.

'Hello, I thought you would be working late tonight.'

'Nah, got it all done.'

'That's great. The boys both got player of the week awards at soccer this afternoon. They'll be so happy to tell you so don't let them know you know.' She is looking at him strangely, really looking at him.

Leo laughs. 'Smart coach,' he says, dropping his eyes from her gaze, staring down at the black and white tiled kitchen floor. There is a chip on one tile and a crack through another. Nothing lasts the way it should.

'I know. I don't think I could have coped with only one of them winning.'

'They'll have to get used to that eventually,' says Leo, his gaze moving over the rest of the floor.

Diana pours herself some wine and takes a sip. 'I realise that. But tonight, I would just like to enjoy the fact that they're both happy to share the award. I would like to enjoy tonight,' she repeats.

Leo nods. 'I'll make a big deal of it.'

Diana is quiet for a moment and he looks up. She is staring at him again in a really disconcerting way.

'Is something wrong?' he asks.

'No, but... you wouldn't believe what happened to me today,' she says.

'What?' he asks.

'Some woman sent me a picture of her breasts, just her breasts and nothing else. At first, I thought it might be a patient asking if she had mastitis because I've had mothers send me pictures before when they're unsure but this is not a picture of a breastfeeding woman's breasts, look.'

Diana pulls her phone out of her pocket and opens it to the picture, turning the screen to Leo.

'I hope she realised she sent it to the wrong phone. If she did the poor thing must be so embarrassed. Can you imagine dating today – naked pictures seem to be part of the deal. I hope she managed to send one to the man or woman who's waiting for it.'

Leo can't breathe in the warm kitchen, his hand trembling a little as he puts the glass of wine down on the marble countertop.

'She didn't send any message with the picture?' he asks.

'Nope, nothing.'

'Why have you kept it?' He turns away and grabs a glass from the cupboard to fill with water, his heart racing.

'I wanted to show you, but I'll delete it now. Imagine if the boys found it.' He watches as she deletes the picture.

Leo drinks deeply, wishing for a whisky, for a double, triple, quadruple whisky. 'Yeah, that would be...' In his pocket, his phone buzzes with a message and he pulls it out, looks at the text he has received.

*Should I tell her who I am?* It's from a number he doesn't recognise but he knows it's from Serena. It's definitely from Serena.

'Work?' asks Diana.

'Yeah... I better just email this client,' he says walking out of the kitchen and going into his study where he closes the door behind him and locks it.

*Why did you do that? How did you get her number?* How did she even know to text him right now? Is Serena watching him? Is the psycho, car-destroying boyfriend following him? He turns to look at the window of his study but the blind is down and unless someone has a camera in his house... No, that's ridiculous.

Adrenalin surges around his body. All of the things he takes for granted, all of the things that bore him, are suddenly at risk. He could lose all this. And he very much would not like to lose this. It feels like it's all he has left right now. What is she playing at? She ended it. Why do this now? She's made sure that the small tattoo of a heart is in the frame, the tendrils surrounding it. But even if he hadn't seen the tattoo, he would know it was her. The fantasy of her body is a place he can't stop his mind from wandering to, especially now that he knows he's never going to see it again.

He holds his phone, staring down at it, willing her reply to come so that he knows just how much danger his whole life is in.

*What do you want?*

He sends the message as he hears Diana call, 'Leo, we're waiting for you.'

**Ten thousand cash.**

A horrified laugh bursts from Leo's lips. This must be a joke. It has to be. Maybe this isn't Serena? Maybe this is some scammer trying their luck? No one else was supposed to know about them but maybe she shared the information. Did someone see them together? That picture was of Serena's breasts. He knows that for sure. She's a successful real estate agent and she doesn't need his money so what is this about? *Maybe she's not who she says she is. Maybe the reason you couldn't find anything on her is because she doesn't actually exist.*

*You don't need my money,* he tries.

'Leo,' Diana calls again.

**Ten thousand cash by tomorrow night. I'll text you where or she hears about every single encounter in every hotel room for the last few weeks.**

'Dad, we have news,' Rowan calls and Leo grits his teeth. He wants to throw his phone against the wall and watch it smash into a thousand pieces. Bitch. Goddamn bitch. Was this the plan all along? Is this what she does? Swan around conferences in a tight dress to hook unsuspecting men so she can blackmail them? He'll kill her, he'll literally kill her. But first he has to get to her and he has no idea where she lives or works. He's such an idiot.

*Fine. Let me know when and where.*

He switches the phone off and slides it into his pocket, his heart racing and a headache tightening around his forehead. *Bitch, bitch, bitch,* he keeps repeating to himself as he leaves his office and joins his family around the kitchen table where the roast chicken is honey brown and the potatoes are crunchy with herbs.

'Guess what, Dad,' says Rowan as Leo tops up his glass of wine and clears his mind of everything else.

She's threatening his family, his life, everything.

He won't let her get away with that. No way.

'What?' asks Leo, and Rowan and Sawyer talk over each other in their eagerness to tell him about the award as Diana smiles and nods while she listens to them.

Leo listens as his mind twists around the problem of Serena. Would she actually tell Diana about the affair and how would Diana react? Maybe this is all some sort of joke? No. She seemed serious and it makes sense when he thinks about it. Serena is twenty-eight and gorgeous. He's forty-three and good-looking enough but he should have been aware he was being played from the first moment they met. There were a lot of richer, better-looking men at that conference and it was just his bad luck that she picked him. How many times has she done this before?

'Leo,' says Diana.

'Yes, that's amazing, boys, you're both so talented, well done. I'm proud of you. Maybe you can both play for the Socceroos when you get older.'

'Yay!!' both boys shout in unison.

Diana smiles and Leo is relieved he has replied appropriately despite tuning out the story. *You're such an idiot,* he tells himself as he pours more wine into his glass and then tops up Diana's glass for her.

Shifting in his seat, he takes a huge mouthful of his drink, trying to drown out the terrible discomfort of humiliation. How is he going to explain taking ten thousand dollars of their savings to Diana? It will almost wipe out their account.

Leo puts a potato in his mouth, savouring the crispy salt on the skin.

Maybe he should refuse to be blackmailed? He can tell Serena to go screw herself and accept the consequences. Diana will ask for a divorce and his family life will disappear but maybe he can survive that? He pictures himself in a small apartment, alone. The image is depressing.

It's easy enough to eat silently while the boys talk about their award, about their day at school, about every single thing that comes to their minds. Life is just an adventure waiting to happen for his kids. What will happen to them if he and Diana get divorced? How will it change them and their futures?

He glances at Diana who laughs at something Rowan says, her eyes lighting up with her love for him. Her eyes used to light up like that when she talked to him.

He has friends who are divorced, men who look old before their time as they constantly check their phones for the schedule of when they can see their kids. He's been envious of friends who are divorced like Graham and Ivan and Joel. But his envy for these men has faded as the years go by. Leo knows that Tinder is like an always open candy shop when you first get out of a marriage but even Graham, who had been married to Valerie for twenty years and had the looks and stamina to keep up with women half his age, eventually started talking about finding someone to settle down with.

'Why?' Leo asked him over a catch-up they had once a month. 'You have everything and you can pick and choose who you spend time with.'

'Mate, I would like to be able to sit next to someone on a sofa and not have to explain my references to songs and television and movies. I want someone who cares if I've had a bad day or if I'm sick. This has been great but I'm bloody tired now.'

And even though he has been aware of all this, Leo has stupidly put his whole life in jeopardy for some great sex. And now he has a choice to make. Is this family, this dinner at a kitchen table, this life, worth ten thousand dollars? Perhaps it is priceless. He can pay the money.

But will ten thousand dollars be the end of it?

As he chews a bite of chicken, seasoned just the way he likes it, he reflects on what has happened to his car and his office. What if this has nothing at all to do with Peter Denton or his drug addict father – what if this is all Serena Burns and her sidekick boyfriend, just as he thought?

If he refuses to get the money to her, will she remind him of what has happened to his car and his office and then tell him that the same thing will happen to him?

The chicken turns rubbery in his mouth and Leo picks up his wine again, draining the glass.

He has no real choice here.

'Bad day?' asks Diana and Leo looks at his wife with her neat ponytail and her slightly flushed cheeks. Why is she looking at him like that?

Leo ducks his head, not wanting her to be able to read his expression. 'The usual shit, you know,' he says.

'Dad, that's not an allowed word in this house,' says Sawyer sternly.

'Sorry, bud,' Leo says. 'I may just finish some work.' He stands up and leaves his unfinished plate on the table before Diana has a chance to say anything and then he goes into his study and closes the door, sitting behind his slim timber desk where his home laptop is. He turns on his phone, his heart racing in anticipation of the message from Serena but there's nothing from her.

How long will he have to wait for a text from Serena and what will happen when it comes? After staring down at his phone for five minutes he sighs and opens his laptop, logging in to his work email.

The top email is from Martin, his boss.

Hi Leo,

We need to speak re this Denton mess. Please talk to Blake and set up a meeting for the two of us.

Martin

Leo wonders if the Denton house could mean the end of his career at Gantry. It's all gotten so out of control and he hasn't even read the email Peter Denton sent the whole agency. The guy is trying to ruin his life. It's not enough that he has to deal with this mad woman he slept with, he also has this coming at him. Reluctantly he finds the agency-wide email sent by Peter Denton.

He needs to know what it says in order to have something to tell Martin. He's been actively avoiding reading it, despite knowing that it's not just going to go away.

To whom it may concern at Gantry Real Estate.

I am writing to inform you that I have engaged legal counsel in order to begin proceedings against Leo Palmer and the agency. My grandmother has been forced into a sale by your agent Leo Palmer and he has, thus far, refused to answer my communications on this matter. He has also failed to find a way to allow this matter to come to a successful resolution.

This is unacceptable business practice and I will be using every legal aspect possible to make sure that Leo Palmer and this agency suffer the consequences of this heinous behaviour.

Peter Denton

Leo drops his head, staring down at his blue suit pants, exhaustion running through his veins. He hates this bloody job. But he needs it. He can only imagine Diana's reaction if he is forced to find another agency. The Sydney real estate market is small and gossipy; everyone will know he's been asked to leave.

With every fibre of his being, he wishes Peter Denton dead. And then just because his anger is burning in his stomach, he wishes Serena dead as well.

Leo indulges himself with a few minutes of self-pity before his father's voice commands him to 'man up'. Leo heard the phrase from the time he was two years old, every time he cried, every time he was upset about something, every time he failed.

Before he can give it any more thought, he emails Peter Denton.

We need to meet.

The reply is so swift it's almost instant.

Yes, we do. Time and place?

Leo doesn't reply. He will wait to hear from Serena and maybe then he can get all this shit over with in one night.

What he does do is go out to his car and find the tyre wrench in his boot, sticking it in the front seat, feeling a surge of adrenalin at what he can do with the arm-length metal pole. Someone hit in the head with it would not get up again too quickly.

*Man up, man up, man up*, he keeps repeating to himself.

And that's what he's going to do.

# EIGHTEEN

## SERENA

Two Days Ago

Late on Friday afternoon, Serena pushes open the door of the Winfield care home and waves at the receptionist, Gemma, who is on the phone, a pencil twirling in her hand. 'He's had a good night,' Serena hears her say to whoever she is talking to. Gemma nods at Serena in reply to her greeting as she keeps talking, her voice low and soothing. The young woman is perfectly suited to this job with her endless patience and reservoir of kindness.

Moving along the plushily carpeted hallway, she reminds herself to take deep breaths. She comes once a week and it's never easy. It will get harder. Dr Chen has advised her of that.

'Your mother is in the end stages of her disease, I'm afraid,' he told her last week, nodding his head as he spoke.

'How long?' Serena asked.

'It is not a matter of how long, my dear,' he said kindly. 'The body can hang on for years but you need to know that she will have to be moved to the acute care section soon. She is not able to be alone for any length of time anymore. She is healthy but needs help with everything now. She forgets to eat and of course you know that she needs help with bathing, with everything.'

Serena had nodded, desperate and sad. Her mother's Alzheimer's began when she was only fifty-five, with repeating herself in the same conversation, forgetting words for simple things, like 'fork', and then getting lost on her daily walks. 'Something is wrong with me,' she'd told her in a moment of clarity. 'Something is wrong and you need to take me to a doctor and then you need to prepare yourself.'

'I'm sure you're fine, Mum, maybe you just need to rest more,' Serena replied but her mother was a nurse and she had laid a hand gently on her daughter's arm and forced Serena to meet her gaze. 'Something is wrong, my darling, and you need to prepare.'

Now Serena knocks and opens the door to her mother's room where she finds her gazing out at the garden, where the liquidambar trees are dropping the last of their leaves. Serena is an adult but she still loves the feeling of crunching through the fallen leaves, reminded of the best times in her childhood home where, after a day of stamping on the leaves, the whole family gathered around the fire, playing board games on a Saturday night as the temperature outside dropped to freezing.

'Hey, Mum,' says Serena, bending down slowly to kiss her mother's cheek.

Her mother turns to look at her and Serena can see the confusion in her eyes. Since Louise has been moved into the care home, there have been moments of clarity, moments when she simply appears again and asks questions about her daughter's life, but it is obvious that today will have none of those moments.

'Darling,' says her mother and Serena's heart lifts because perhaps she is wrong about the unfocused stare her mother is giving her.

'Yes, Mum?'

'I'm so glad you haven't left for school yet. Matty forgot his lunch. Can you take it to him for me?'

Serena blinks rapidly, forcing away the tears that appear. 'Yep, sure.'

'I know it's annoying, love, but he needs to eat. Silly boy.' Her mother smiles and turns back to the window, watching two people walk through the garden, bundled up in puffer coats and beanies.

Serena drops into a chair next to her mother and studies the moving figures, wondering who they are.

'I saw Leo,' Serena says now.

'Leo,' repeats her mother although Serena doesn't think she has any idea of who Leo is but there is some comfort in that.

Every week since her meetings with Leo began, Serena has told her mother about them, about what she is doing. She confesses her dislike of the man and of herself, and her mother listens and then forgets and, somehow, it is easier to keep going after that.

'It's nearly over, which is good.'

'Well, you don't like him,' says her mother with a small smile. 'He pulls your hair.'

Serena nods, knowing that her mother is referring to a boy from year two named Bently who used to pull her neatly done plaits every lunch until Serena punched him in the nose. She was sent to the principal's office and her mother called and when she came, still dressed in her scrubs from her shift at the hospital, Louise listened to the story and then said, 'So what you object to is that my daughter, my seven-year-old child, who has repeatedly told her teacher that she is being harassed by this little menace, defended herself. Is that the problem?'

'No... well, not really it's just—' began her principal, Mr Hattersley.

'Because young women need to be taught from a very early

age to defend themselves, especially in this day and age. I hope you are not objecting to that.'

Bently never pulled her hair again and Serena grew up with a core belief in her own strength and power, in her ability to defend herself and control her life until tragedy forced her to question everything.

'I feel like a bad person, Mum, like a really bad person. He's married and I shouldn't be doing this,' Serena whispers.

Her mother turns from the window and smiles at her. 'You won't forget Matty's lunch, will you? I might have a nap before my shift but don't forget, will you?'

Serena stands and sighs. 'Of course not, Mum, I have it. Do you want me to help you to your bed?'

'Oh no, sweetheart, I'm watching them, the man and his father.' She gestures towards the two figures in the garden.

'Do you know who they are?'

'I think the man's name is Leo – you don't like Leo, do you?'

Serena sighs, takes another deep breath, prays for patience. She wishes she were a better person but it's been a long day. She needs to go home and sit on her sofa, drink a glass of wine and put everything out of her mind for a bit. 'I'll see you soon,' she says and her mother nods, her interest on the figures in the garden.

'Don't forget Matty's lunch. I made him roast beef and salad; he likes that.'

Serena nods, unable to stop her tears. She blinks rapidly. 'I'll take it to him now,' she says, kissing her mother again.

'Melanie Serena,' says her mother as she opens the door to leave.

'Yes, Mum,' she answers. When she was younger, her mother's use of her full name usually meant she was in line for a lecture over some transgression. But now when her mother uses it, she experiences a jolt of joy at this evidence of her mother remembering, of her mother still being here.

'Thank you, my darling, for everything you're doing. Thank you,' and then she turns back to the window.

'I love you, Mum,' she whispers. But her mother doesn't reply.

She could have chosen any old name to use when she saw Leo. But she needed to have something of herself to hold onto. If she couldn't be Melanie and she couldn't use her real surname, then she needed to be Serena, her middle name and her late grandmother's name. Serena would sleep with Leo, would manipulate Leo, would make Leo pay for what he had done. Melanie Serena would remain separate, would preserve who she truly was.

In the car she allows herself five minutes for tears but only five minutes.

As she begins her drive home, she lets herself think about her brother Matty who always forgot his lunch. Once Melanie Serena entered high school, she was put in charge of delivering it to him and she remembers that even though she had always rolled her eyes and complained about having to find him and give him the square blue Tupperware filled with two sand-wiches, fruit and junk food, she always got a slight thrill out of it.

Matty was tall with red hair from their father and brown eyes from their mother and a cheeky smile. Lots of red-headed children were teased but Matty was loved by everyone from the janitor at the school to the teachers to the students and when she did find him at his favourite hangout near the canteen, he was always glad to see her, always grateful for his lunch. 'Ah, it's my little angel sister,' he would say as he saw her, 'bringing me my lunch. Everyone, say thanks to little sis for keeping me fed so I don't get hangry,' he would laugh and his group of friends would good-naturedly chorus, 'Thanks, little sis.' It always made her feel special.

Having to tell her mother over and again that Matty is gone, that he has been gone for a long time, slices through her each and every time she has to do it. That's why she no longer does it. It serves no purpose.

It is easier to let Matty be alive and well. Easier to have him permanently waiting for her by the canteen, a grin on his face.

'I'm doing this for you, Matty,' she whispers and she hopes that he can hear her, that he's watching over her, and that even though she is doing something he wouldn't agree with, he understands.

This will be done soon. And then she will be able to tell her mother about Matty being gone for the final time and that she has meted out the correct punishment for this terrible crime.

That's what she will tell her mother and then she will let her retreat back into the past where Matty is waiting at the canteen for his lunch.

Everything is in place now, ready to go, and the plan is solid. She's not done with Leo Palmer. Not by a long shot.

# PART TWO

EIGHT MONTHS AGO

# NINETEEN

## MELANIE

Sunday 10 December

Melanie takes a small sip of water, trying to quell her churning stomach as she stares down at her mobile phone. It's going to ring any minute now. Any minute now.

She could just not answer it. No one is forcing her to take the call. She is sitting in an armchair made from blue velvet, a chair she loves because it was expensive and she had saved up for it, had looked at it in the store window for weeks every time she walked past and had finally bought it and has loved it ever since.

Looking around her small apartment she wonders why she ever agreed to the call. This space is her space, her safe space, from the expensive chair to the much cheaper cream and blue rug and the small kitchen with white marble benchtops. A huge chunk of her salary goes into paying the mortgage every month but it's a sacrifice she's prepared to make because the one-bedroom space is hers and hers alone and when she closes the door at night, she shuts out her job and the rest of the world.

But now she's going to let *him*, the caller, in here, allow him to invade her space and she could have just said, 'no.'

But she didn't. And she knows it's because, even though she can look around her apartment and see the things she has acquired that are supposed to make her feel like an adult, like the coffee machine bought at the Boxing Day sales and the file holding all her insurance and bank papers and the keys to her own apartment with a parking space, she still doesn't feel like an adult. Instead, she feels like she stopped at nineteen years old. She is stuck at nineteen because that's when it happened. And even though those around her may believe she's moved on, even though she has a job and a car and an apartment and friends, she's still that nineteen-year-old girl. Still that girl who was woken by the sound of her mother's screams late on a Friday night, only to sit up in bed and see the flashing blue and red lights of a police car in their driveway. She's still there, stuck in that moment of knowing something terrible had happened but not knowing just how terrible it was.

That night she went to bed, thinking about an assignment for university, and she woke up to a police car in the driveway and two policemen on the doorstep, with their hats in their hands, there to tell her family that Matthew, Matty, was gone.

And she's been here ever since, existing in parallel with the Melanie who is getting on with her life. It feels like she's never wholly anywhere at all. She is never completely at work, never totally engrossed in a book or a movie, never absolutely present with the few girlfriends she has. Even dating feels wrong, as though she shouldn't be doing anything that could bring love and pleasure and possibly a family of her own into her life.

And some part of her hopes that by talking to the caller, by listening to him, she will somehow find a way to become unstuck.

She lays the phone on her lap, wipes her clammy hands on

her Lycra leggings. She will go running after the call. She will need to.

Her brown hair is tied back and her face is free of make-up, and she knows that there are shadows under her brown eyes. She didn't sleep at all last night.

Four weeks ago, an email came through the public prosecutor's office, from the lawyer who had represented the state years ago, a man that Melanie still kept in touch with through occasional emails. He was an older man, worn down by his job of prosecuting the worst criminals in Australia, but incredibly kind and interested in Melanie and her family.

> Hi Melanie. I hope you're well. I received this from his lawyer and thought I would send it to you to deal with. You're under no obligation at all. You can communicate directly with his lawyer if you would like to go ahead. Let me know if you want to talk about this. Dan.

She hadn't understood at first until she scrolled down, her eyes scanning the words. But then one sentence stood out as though written in giant bold letters.

**Would you be open to a phone call from him?**

No. That was her immediate reaction. No, she would not speak to him. No, she did not want to hear his voice. Not after all this time.

And then she thought about it, slept on it, let it circle in her mind. The emphatic 'no' became a 'maybe'. What could he want to say to her? What could he possibly say to her? And what could she bear to hear? She emailed his lawyer and asked what he wanted but his lawyer had no idea.

In the end she agreed.

He had a number, a Prisoner MIN, master index number,

366933. And before she agreed to the call, she made a decision. That's how she would think of him. He would not be a man with a name, not a person, not a human being, but a number. He was a thing and therefore, whatever he had to say couldn't touch her, hurt her. She would listen to the number as she would an automated recording.

In her lap, the phone trills, startling her so she jumps and drops it and then has to scrabble for it on the carpet, her fingers sliding across the screen twice until it works.

'Yes, hello?'

*'This is a call from Long Vale Correctional Facility. Are you prepared to accept the call from...'* Melanie doesn't listen to his name, just thinks of his number, which she has now memorised from repeated readings of the email.

'Yes,' she says, loudly, too loudly.

'Hi Melanie?' His voice is shockingly normal. This is an everyday conversation, his tone seems to imply. She considers hanging up immediately.

Instead, she takes a deep breath, 'Yes, hi, hi. Um hi.'

'I didn't think it would actually be you,' he says, relief obvious now. 'I mean, I know you said you would accept my call in the message you sent through my lawyer but I didn't think you would.'

'I wasn't sure I should. I didn't... I wasn't going to and then I thought... I wanted to know what you had to say.'

'I am so grateful that you did accept the call. Just letting you know that calls are timed here so I may have to get off the phone and everything is recorded.' He speaks fast.

'How long do we have?'

'Six minutes?'

'Six minutes? That's... wow.' *Idiot*, she curses herself, *what a stupid thing to say*. But why should she care if he thinks she's an idiot? He's the one in prison.

'It's prison,' he sighs.

Melanie bites her lip, unsure what to say.

'Do you have any questions for me? Anything you want to ask?'

'I have a million questions,' she says curtly, 'but I wasn't the one who wanted to talk. What do you want to say to me?'

He waits a beat of his precious minutes and then says, 'I'm... going to be very honest here. I'm coming up for parole.'

'Parole?'

'Yes. I was sentenced to a minimum of eight years and I've served eight years if they include the time served before the trial, which they do. My actual sentence was ten years but I can get parole now.'

The heat of fury rises up from her toes, burning up through her legs and into her churning stomach. 'Just like that? You get out early just like that?' she yells.

'No... no, not just like that, not, not, not at all.' He trips over the words. 'It's a whole process and it's taken me months to get to this point. And I have to have shown... I have to have proved... Look, I know it's not what you wanted to hear but please don't hang up, please.'

She has moved the phone away from her ear, is staring down at the red handset icon that will end the call. How had he known? 'Why have you called me? What do you want? What exactly do you want?' she spits, bringing it closer to her ear again.

'God,' he agonises, 'this is not how this was supposed to go. I want to talk to you about my parole. They will contact you anyway because you have a right to... tell them that you don't want me to be released.'

Melanie turns her free hand into a fist, hits down on her leg, letting the tiny shock of pain distract her. She can hear him breathing fast, panting almost, as though panicked.

'Then that's what I'll do... that's what I'll do because—' she says, enjoying the power of her words.

'Oh please, please,' he interrupts her, 'just give me a chance. I promise if you still want me in jail after we talk, I'll accept that. I'll just accept that you'll tell them not to let me out.'

Melanie is suddenly exhausted. Rage and hate take so much energy. 'Can I stop them letting you out? Do they care what I think?'

'They do, but more importantly, I do. You may not be able to stop my parole, but they do take what you want into account. Your family are victims and you have a right to tell them how you feel.'

There is a clatter of sound, like metal hitting metal, and someone shouts, swears and then raucous laughter.

'Why it so noisy there?'

'There are a lot of guys waiting for their turn. I don't have long, Melanie. Please just ask me something, ask me anything. Just don't hang up, okay, please don't hang up.'

The question appears without Melanie giving it much thought. 'Okay, here's a question, my first question. Do you think about him, about my brother, about Matthew?'

'I do... all the time.'

Melanie doesn't even try to hide her snort of derision.

'You're not sure if you can believe me, are you?'

'I don't know you. I don't know anything about you except what was said at trial and I have to say that I've just... put a lot of that out of my mind.' She knows this is a lie, but she doesn't owe him the truth. She doesn't owe him anything. 'I don't want to think about you at all. I don't want to ever think about you again. Do you know how hard I've worked to never have to even consider you at all?'

'I understand. I completely understand but you said you would accept my call.'

'Yes, I did. Now answer my question. Do you think about him?'

'You need to believe me when I say that I think about him

every single day. I see his face every day. I see it when I look at my own face in the mirror and I think about how he doesn't get to do that, to see himself in a mirror. When I shave, I think about how he doesn't get to do that. Yesterday I ate an orange after lunch and it was bitter, not sweet, and I think it's maybe because it's not really the season for oranges. They're more a winter fruit but when the acid hit my tongue, I thought of Matthew. I thought about how he would never get to have that experience again.'

Her anger and scepticism morph instantly into terrible grief and tears choke her. 'Matty loved oranges,' she manages to say.

'Oh, you're crying, please don't cry. I didn't mean to make you cry.' He sounds genuinely distraught but she doesn't know if he actually feels upset. He's a number. Numbers can't feel.

But whatever he feels, she doesn't want him to hear her cry. 'No, it's fine... I like to think about the good stuff, about the stuff he loved. I like to think about that now. It took me a long time to get here.' She wants to take back the statement instantly. Why is she telling him anything about herself?

A few short beeps intrude into the silence. 'What are those beeps?'

'It means we're out of time, shit.'

'That's fine.' It's over now and it's done. She managed it.

'Can I call again next week? I only get one call a week so can I call you again? Would that be okay?' he asks quickly, desperately.

'No! I mean, I don't know...'

'Please, please say yes.'

'You can call but I don't know. I just don't know if I can speak to you again.' She won't accept the call next week. She knows she won't.

'Okay, thank you, thank—' and then there is silence. He's gone.

Melanie sits back in her chair and then immediately

forward again when she feels her shirt is damp. She has sweated through her running shirt as though she has already run.

She doesn't have to speak to him ever again. He can get parole or not. He can rot in jail, he can die. She stands and gets her cap, her ear buds and her key and, in less than a minute, she is out on the street in the sunshine, her feet taking her on their usual route.

She doesn't have to take the call, doesn't have to take the call, doesn't have to take the call.

But she probably will.

# TWENTY

## MELANIE

Sunday 17 December

She's not as nervous about the call this week, not as unsure. Once again, she has gone round and around telling herself that she does not have to accept the call or speak to him ever again but if she is going to try and stop his parole, she needs something, some ammunition against him. She has been distracted at work and last night, out with her friend, Vicky, she hadn't exactly been good company.

'Do you want to talk about it?' Vicky asked after ten minutes of silence.

'I'm sorry,' Melanie replied, taking a huge gulp of her wine as she looked around the Mexican restaurant where large groups of people were talking and laughing. 'It's just a lot of noise.'

'We can go somewhere else, just talk,' said Vicky, her dark eyes searching Melanie's face.

'No, no, it's nothing... just a bad day.'

Vicky smiled. 'I think what you need is a good date.'

'I'm good, thank you – don't you go fixing me up with any more of your cousins,' laughed Melanie. Vicky came from a large extended family of very good-looking men but Melanie couldn't seem to get past the first few dates with anyone, let alone one of Vicky's cousins, and she couldn't explain the reason to Vicky, not in a way that she would understand. Melanie had only met Vicky after Matthew died. She was sympathetic but it was the past and not something Melanie discussed often. Another two glasses of wine had allowed her to push the phone call to the back of her mind until this morning when the dread had begun circling again.

When the phone rings she takes a deep breath and answers, listens to the automated voice asking her if she will accept the call. 'Yes,' she says and then, 'Hello?'

'Hi, thanks for accepting the call again. I really appreciate it,' he says casually, too casually.

The ever-present simmering anger rears up inside her. 'It's... it's whatever. I don't know how I'm supposed to respond to you. Do you know how hard this is for me?' She fails to moderate her voice but she doesn't care.

'I do, I do, I'm sorry, please don't yell. I'm sorry,' he says, contrite and desperate again. 'I know you were angry last week about why I wanted to talk to you. I know this is hard for you. I understand.'

Melanie leans down and looks at her sneakers, concentrating on their pink and purple stripes, not colours she has ever chosen before but they make her smile when she looks at them. 'I really don't think you do. You're in prison because you killed my brother. You destroyed my family and now you want me to help you.' She sits up again, stands and walks to her balcony door where she can look out at the park opposite her apartment. 'It's just... it's ridiculous,' she says forcefully.

'I'm begging you, begging you to not hang up,' he whispers as though embarrassed to be saying the words and she remembers that he is in a public place with other people waiting to use the phone. 'Please, please—'

'I won't hang up. Okay, just calm down. I won't.'

'Thank you, thank you.'

Melanie gazes out at the people in the park, watches a man she has seen before running. He does four laps of the large park every Sunday. 'I did... I did start thinking about the trial, remembering things, I guess.'

'What did you remember?' he asks softly.

'I remember that you wanted to say something, to tell us something more but your lawyer wouldn't let you say it. He just shut you down whenever you did more than just answer a question directly. I felt like you were hiding something but also that you didn't want to hide it anymore.' She watches the man as he runs around a bend and disappears for a while but she knows he'll be back.

'There was stuff I wanted to say, stuff I told the police and my lawyer but they said it would hurt my case.'

'Do you want to tell me now? I mean... I'll listen, is what I'm saying.'

'I... they record these calls. The important thing is that I've served my time for what I did and I wanted to ask you not to block my parole.'

Melanie can hear that there is something more, a lot more, but she swallows down her questions because he's right, this call is being recorded so he's not going to say anything that could jeopardise his parole.

'You have been there for a long time. That's what I keep reminding myself.' And it's true, she does remind herself of that. In eight years, her whole life has changed.

'And I've felt every day of my eight-year sentence, I have.'

'That's what prison is for,' she says harshly.

'Listen, Melanie,' he sighs, 'I think you're a good person. Only a good person would accept a call from the man who killed her brother. And because you are a good person, I think that you'll give me a chance to prove to you that I've done my time and I deserve to be released.'

Just under a month ago, before she was contacted by the prosecutor and his lawyer, Melanie had days, whole days where she did not think about Matthew. She didn't think about how he died, about whether or not he was scared at the end, if he knew. She didn't think about her mother's devastating heartbreak, about the feeling of no longer being a family. But now she is thinking about it all the time. She is right back where she was nine years ago, struggling to concentrate on anything else. She has a hundred questions for this man in jail, for this murderer. 'You know,' she says, 'I started thinking about the last day of the trial, the day when the jury made their decision. We'd been outside, just waiting in the sun, and finally they called us and we all filed back into court.'

'I will never forget that day,' he says. 'It was hot, just like today, although it was probably a lot hotter because it was the end of February.'

'Yes, hot, and when we were waiting, my mum told me she wanted a milkshake. It was a weird thing for her to ask for but I realised that it was the first time she'd had something sweet since Matty died. Like she'd been depriving herself of what she loved until the trial was over, until she got...'

'Justice. Is that what you were going to say – justice?'

'I guess. People need to pay for their crimes. You needed to pay for your crime.' She doesn't tell him that she would like him to go on paying for the rest of his life. Even without parole he will be out in two years. It's not enough. Nothing could ever be enough.

'But what if...?' he starts to ask and then stops.

Melanie bites her lip, irritated. 'So can I be honest with you?' She doesn't want to talk to him if he's going to question the decision made by the jury.

'Of course.'

'I don't really want to hear about how justice wasn't served or that you weren't in your right mind because if that's what you're going to tell me, I don't want to hear it. You were found guilty. My brother is dead and I don't want to speak to you if all you're planning to do is deny that you are responsible. Because if that's how you feel after all these years, then you should not get parole, you should stay in prison.'

'Okay... okay, please don't get upset, don't get upset.'

She wants to tell him that she's tired of him saying that. The very nature of this conversation is upsetting, everything about this is upsetting and yet she cannot seem to just hang up and ignore this man forever. She is waiting for something, listening for something but she's not sure what. 'I don't see how I can react any other way to what you just said. But I've been thinking about this all week. You've been in prison for eight years. If you are released it won't bring Matty back, and if you're not released it won't bring Matty back, and I know that people deserve a second chance. I'm a big believer in that, really.' This is the truth. She has always felt this way. Why send people to prison if you do not believe that reform is possible? And yet when it has become personal, when it is her family broken, her life altered, she has found it hard to hold onto that belief.

'Okay, tell me what you want to know, tell me what you need to know so that you won't stop me from getting parole. I won't say anything about the case. I'm just grateful to get a chance to speak to you. So tell me what you need to hear.'

Melanie asks the question that has been buzzing around her mind since the first call, since the noise she could hear in the background, making it clear where the call was coming from. 'Can you tell me what it's like there, what it's been like for you?'

'You want to know if I've suffered enough?'

Melanie doesn't answer, surprised by his perception.

'Don't answer that, it's fine. So when you say what it's like, do you mean every day?'

'Well, kind of. Were you scared when you first went in, when you first got there?'

'Terrified. Absolutely terrified. I mean... I didn't sit down at meal times for a month, I just stood on the side holding my tray because I wasn't sure where to sit without pissing someone off. I just didn't know what to do so I would lean against the wall and gulp my food as fast as I could so that I could just get out of there and go back to my cell.'

The flash of sympathy she feels surprises her. It feels wrong. She should not feel anything except contempt and anger, hate and rage towards this man. But he was very young when he went to prison, only a year older than she was at the time. He was regarded as a man by law but he had barely left boyhood behind.

'Oh, that's... awful. But you haven't done that for eight years, have you?'

'Nah, some guy... a guy named Adam, took pity on me. One morning he came up to me and he was a big guy, like really big, and he said, "sit here" and he pointed at his table. I thought he was going to do something... do something to me, like make me into his... God, I don't even want to think about it. But it was obvious that I had no choice in the matter. I'd seen what happened to guys who didn't do what they were told by those who hold the power in prison, and I don't mean the guards. It's a whole world in here and... just hang on a second... This is my time and I swear to God if you don't just back the hell away now,' he growls. 'Sorry, I'm back... people get impatient when it's phone call time. What was I saying?'

The switch in his voice is unnerving. When he speaks to those around him it's filled with aggression but his tone changes completely when he speaks to her again.

'Um... You were telling me about this guy named Adam who told you to sit at his table. So what happened?'

'Nothing, I just sat there and ate my breakfast and he didn't say anything at all but at lunch he came up to me again and said, "sit here" and then he told me that I could sit with him every meal. I think he felt sorry for me. I was only just twenty and I was so skinny and permanently shaking. I must have looked like I was going to have some kind of breakdown.'

'That was nice of him, to help you.' She struggles to imagine the world of the prison, images coming to her from television series. Is it really like that?

'It was and he started talking to me, just telling me how to get through my years. He told me to start lifting weights because he said it was a way to pass the time, to know that time was passing. The bigger you get, the more time has passed.'

'And is he still there? Do you still sit with him?'

'No, he left after six months but by then I was able to kind of function. I got into it a few times over the years when someone thought I needed a smack. I'd never been hit before prison, never even been in a fight. I spent most of my teenage years actively avoiding confrontation.'

'You sound so... I don't know, blasé about it all,' she says.

'I don't mean to sound like that because it's not okay. I don't want you to think that. Nothing about being in here has been okay. I've marked off every day on a calendar on my wall and each time I get a new calendar because a whole year has passed, it takes me just like... days to accept where I am. I don't want to get another calendar in here.'

She hates that he's brought the conversation back to his parole, smoothly sliding it into the conversation. She feels like he's gaslighting her, telling her what she wants to hear rather than the truth. 'Maybe that's not my concern,' she says curtly.

'Maybe not. But you seem to want to understand so I'll keep talking until you want me to tell you something else.'

'Okay. What else do you do? What else happens during the day there... oh God, there's the beeps.'

'I know, sorry. I'll call again next week. Pick up, okay? Please accept the call.'

'I don't know... I...'

She stops speaking because it's obvious he's gone. She doesn't know if she can do this again and yet, somehow, she thinks she will. There are questions she wants to ask, terrible questions but ones that she needs the answers to. Maybe when these conversations are done, when he has his parole and he's out in the world, she won't think about killing him every single day if she knows more about what he's dealt with in prison, if she feels like he's tried to make up for what he did. Because right now she is thinking about killing him, is actually thinking about it, shocking herself with the violent impulse. And that's not how she sees herself, not how she can allow herself to be. She needs to know that he has tried to redeem himself, that he has suffered and been punished and has changed. So she'll take the call next week but now she'll go running, in the heat, in the park, with thoughts of Matty in her head.

# TWENTY-ONE

Sunday, 24 December

'Hi Melanie?'

'Yes, hi,' she replies, glad that his voice no longer makes her heart race. She's getting better at keeping herself calm when she speaks to him. Outside, the December sun is high in a bright-blue sky and a hum of happiness seems to permeate the air. Melanie used to love Christmas time before Matty died, her childish excitement lingering until the first Christmas without him. Now she just wants it done as quickly as possible.

'I wasn't sure I would be able to speak to you today,' he says.

'Because it's Christmas Eve?'

'Yeah, I mean it's still early but I wasn't sure if you would be with your family.'

Melanie thinks about the word 'family' coming out of this man's mouth after what he has done to hers, feels the anger rise inside her but it is instantly quashed by the grief that always intensifies around this time of year.

She sighs. 'I will be, later. I'll be with my mum. But... we haven't really celebrated Christmas since Matty died. I mean we get together and we talk about him, as much as she can remember.'

'She can't remember him?' he asks, shock obvious in his tone.

Melanie is standing on her balcony in the warm air, watching children play in the packed park, their shrieks of joy rising up to her sixth-floor apartment. She wishes she could take the last sentence back. 'She has... I don't want to talk about that,' she says shortly.

'Oh... I'm so sorry... I don't know what to say.' He sounds sorry, but is he?

'It's fine. She hasn't been well since my brother was murdered. Let's just leave it at that.'

'Maybe I should... go.'

Melanie doesn't immediately reply, lets the silence between them grow, eating up the time. She watches a brother and sister who look to be close in age fighting over a bucket and spade in the sandpit, remembers having exactly the same tussle with Matty on a beach. Eventually she hit him and got the bucket. Matty didn't cry, didn't even tell on her, just waited patiently for her to finish playing and hand him the bucket and spade. He was only seven but that's who he was for the rest of his short life. He was kind and patient and always thought of others before he thought of himself. His funeral was huge, with people spilling out of the church as those who knew him and everyone in her family came along to pay their respects. 'Only the good die young,' she heard from more than one well-meaning person. She had wanted to scream when she heard those words, wanted to curse God and swear at whoever had uttered them. Matty was so good and she felt, in the absence of her brother, that she was filled with everything bad and terrible, that she was choking on the ugliness of her dark grief inside her.

Melanie feels tears on her cheeks. Why is she doing this to herself? Why is she letting this man do this to her? 'Do *you* want to go?' she asks scathingly. 'Does it hurt to be called a murderer? Do you not want to acknowledge the truth? I mean you have to do that in order to get parole, don't you?'

'I do. And I acknowledge it but it's not that simple. There is a lot more to this. But if this is too much, if it's too hard, I will never call again. You don't have to speak to me.'

Melanie turns away from the park and walks back inside her apartment, makes her way to the fridge where she has a bottle of wine open. She would gulp it down if she wasn't going for a run. She fills a glass with water instead and holds it, unable to bring herself to swallow anything.

'I can put down the phone, Melanie. Do you want me to leave you alone? I'll do whatever you want.' He is so calm, his voice barely above a whisper, and inside her, something settles. She is letting him call her and there is no point in just yelling at him.

'No wait. I'm sorry I yelled.' She takes a small sip of the water and puts the glass down on the counter, leaning against it and looking around her apartment. Her gaze settles on a photograph of her whole family at her sixteenth birthday party, all of them wearing silly hats and large grins.

'I'm sorry about your mother, about everything, but I'm really sorry that you're going through this now.'

'Thank you,' she whispers and then she shakes her head. 'Anyway, we will meet tonight and talk but it won't be Christmas like we used to have.'

'I bet you had the best Christmases when you were a kid.'

'Why do you say that?'

'Because at the trial you looked like a nice family, a broken one because of what happened but really nice. You and your mother held hands, the whole time. I liked seeing that. I liked that you were so caring of her.'

'Well, she's my mother.' Melanie moves to her sofa, sitting down and leaning her head back.

'Yeah, but not everyone is close to their mother. I'm not.'

Melanie remembers this about him, is surprised she had forgotten. 'I know. I remember that from the trial. I remember them talking about your childhood. I'm sorry your mum was not... a good person. That must have been hard.' Another small tug of sympathy for him pulls at her. She doesn't want this man to make her feel sorry for him, that's not what she's going to do, but he did have a terrible childhood. She remembers that.

'You can get used to anything. I got used to her and the way she treated me.'

She can't let him keep talking about this because it feels like an excuse and she will not tolerate an excuse. She needs to take the conversation in the direction she wants it to go.

'I wanted to ask you about that night, the night Matty died. I want to know what happened,' she says firmly.

'You heard it at the trial.'

'I want to hear it again, from you, just you speaking, not you answering questions from the prosecutor and your lawyer.' She had heard what he said at the trial but most of it has slipped or been pushed from her mind.

'Are you sure about this? I didn't think you would want to hear about it again. I wanted to tell you that I was sorry, that I would never forget Matthew.'

'And you wanted to ask me not to block your parole. Since these conversations are recorded, it would benefit you to tell me what happened and take responsibility. And I want to hear about it, so talk,' she spits. Why is she doing this to herself? Why does she want to hear the words that are going to hurt so much?

'You're angry. I'm sorry.'

'I'm tired. Just tell me so I can listen and not have to speak to you again.' She doesn't really want to hear what happened that night, not again, but at the exact same time, for some reason, she needs to hear it. It will make it easier to write a letter asking for him not to be released. It will make it easier to tell whoever needs to know that she doesn't believe he's reformed at all.

'Okay... okay, here goes. Nine and a half years ago, I had a long day at work and then I went for a drink. I drove my car to the pub where I had dinner and a beer. And then I had another beer and another and another. I don't know how many I actually had but I know that I was drunk. I should have caught a cab home. I should have called someone to pick me up. But I didn't. Instead, I got into my car and I drove.

'At an intersection, I thought the light was green or maybe I thought it was green and then orange or maybe... I was drunk.

'I drove through. I drove fast and I hit a car being driven by someone who had right of way. I hit the car from the side at speed. It was an older car, red. I slammed on the brakes right before I hit it, but it was too late. It was late and there was no one else around.

'After we collided, after the screeching of my tyres and... the crunch of metal and... shattering of glass, I sat in my car for some time before I understood what had happened and then I kind of felt my body, you know the way you do after a fall or an accident, I kind of took inventory to see if I was okay. And when I realised I was fine, I got out of my car – I had to push the door because it was stuck but I managed to get it open. And then I went over to the other car. The other old car where there wasn't an airbag. Where there was a young man, a boy really, and I knew instantly that he was dead. His eyes were open and he was... he was dead.' It's a recitation of facts, spoken quickly. No feeling, no thought, words that he's obviously said over and again, rehearsed and perfected. The small sip of water she has just drunk threatens to come up again.

'Okay, I can't... I can't. I can't listen to this. Sorry, I have to go.'

She hangs up the phone and runs for the bathroom. Afterwards, despite her stomach still churning and the heat outside, she slips on her sneakers and leaves for her run. She will exhaust her body and hopefully that will exhaust her mind. She should never have agreed to these calls. She needs to stop now because it's awful, just awful, and she never wants to speak to him again. She will refuse next week. She will definitely refuse to speak to him ever again.

What did she think she was going to hear? What could he have said that would help?

Nothing. There is nothing that he can say or do.

He could die. He could do that and then the score would be even. Then she would never have to think about him again. He could just die.

# TWENTY-TWO

## MELANIE

Sunday, 31 December

When her phone rings she stares down at it, counting. If it stops after five rings, then she isn't meant to answer it and that's good. But it keeps going as she rocks on her soft leather sofa, her hands under her legs. She's made a deal with herself – ten rings and she will answer but she hadn't imagined how quickly it would get there. And then it's over, ten rings and still, it's ringing. She answers but doesn't say anything, just listens to the automated voice and then whispers quietly, almost too quietly to hear, 'Yes.'

'Hi, are you there?' he asks, his tone unsure.

'I'm here,' she answers, wishing she had given herself fifteen or even twenty rings before she had to pick up.

'I'm sorry about last week. I'm sorry I told you those things. I shouldn't have.'

'I asked. It's done now.' She tries to picture him standing by a phone with a line of other inmates behind him. In her mind his face is fuzzy. She remembers a skinny young man with dark hair who hung his head in court, only daring to look up now and again. They locked eyes once. He looked up and she was staring straight at him and she saw, in his blue eyes, a flash of fear, as though she had the power to hurt him. Can she hurt him now? Can she actually make them keep him in prison?

'I could have found a better way to say it.' His voice is deep, pleasant to listen to, just a man's voice. How can he be the person who destroyed her family?

'You know my mum asked to see the pictures they took of the scene, of his car... everything, but I could never look at it.'

'I understand that. I'm really, really sorry.'

He is sincere. For the first time since they have started talking, she doesn't question this. 'Let's just... I asked and I wasn't ready. But I know there's more to say and I do have more questions.'

'Okay. How was your Christmas? Is it okay for me to ask that? You don't have to answer.'

'It was quiet, as I told you. A small family gathering. But Mum was pretty good. She seemed to enjoy the food and I bought her a cream that smells like coconut, and she remembered a summer holiday we had. We went to a hotel by the beach and it was... it was one of those holidays you never forget. She even remembered Matty learning to surf and getting dunked by a wave. Sorry. I have no idea why I'm telling you this.'

'It's okay, I like... well, not like... but I want to hear more about him.'

'Why?' Melanie asks. If she was the one who had killed someone, she would never want to think about that person again. She would want to run, to hide from the truth of her crimes.

'Sometimes it's easier to not think about the people you hurt, to just put them in a box. It's an us and them kind of thing. I've met a lot of people in here who do that. They kind of turn their victims into less than human so they can cope with what they've done and it's easy to do if you know very little about the person you hurt. I don't want to do that. I want to know more about him, not less.'

'Because you think that will help with parole?' she snaps.

'I've made you angry again. I didn't mean to. I'm aiming for parole but I'm also aiming to be a better human being when I get out of prison.'

Again, she is convinced that he is sincere, that he actually means what he's saying. Forgiveness is such a simple word but such an impossible action. She wants to hate the man on the other end of the phone and yet, the more they speak, the more human he becomes, and the less possible blanket-hate is. She realises that she has done just what he has said others in prison do, she has tried to make him into less than human so she doesn't have to think of him as anything but a murderer. So she can justify her fantasies about him dying. That has worked for the last eight, nearly nine years but it doesn't seem to be working anymore. She is speaking to a man, a person, someone with feelings. 'Can you tell me how you knew... knew he was dead, why you didn't try CPR or something? How come you were so sure?' she asks. The question has been circling in her mind since it happened as she tries to reimagine the scene, seeing Matty being pulled from the car and given CPR, seeing the miracle of his heartbeat returning and then imagining her family standing around his hospital bed as they thank God that he is still with them. The fantasy is at once a comfort and completely devastating.

He takes a breath before he speaks. 'It was just completely obvious. The idea of a soul, of a person having a soul is not something I've given a lot of thought to, or I hadn't until what happened. But when I saw him, I could see that his soul, what-ever made him who he was, was gone. I never imagined that something like that would be so clear. I'm sort of religious and sort of not so it shocked me – that it was so clear.' The words emerge slowly, measured and thoughtful. He doesn't want to upset her again and she can feel that.

'So there was no chance of saving him?'

'There wasn't. I felt for a pulse and it was only a few minutes between me getting out of the car to check on him and the trucker stopping and he seemed to understand that Matthew was, was gone. It wasn't a question. I would have given anything to have been able to save him.'

'Anything?' she asks because this is what she has thought over and again. She would have given anything to save him.

'Absolutely anything.'

'How can you be sort of religious and sort of not?'

'I guess I wasn't then. I was only twenty and I hadn't given it much thought. But I have now. I joined the bible group here because it's something to do, something that passes the time but, actually I kind of like it.'

She wonders if this is a ploy but instantly dismisses the idea. She cannot speak to him anymore if she is just going to question every single sentence. 'Why, what do you like about it?'

'I like the stories. Last week we talked about the story of Jonah and the whale. We discussed how we are all Jonahs in here, and all in the belly of our personal whales. We all have to find faith in ourselves and in God and keep believing that we will get to a better place. Bible group has made me more aware that there is something out there, something greater than all of us but I never went to church growing up or anything like that.'

'Oh, that's good, I guess.'

'It's... what it is, and you should know that he died immediately. He died immediately. I believe that with all my heart. He didn't suffer but he left behind a family who loved him and they – you – have suffered every day that he is not in this world.'

Melanie cannot speak but she nods as her eyes fill with tears.

'I wrote some other stuff for the psychologist about how I

see your brother's face in my nightmares and how much I regret everything that happened...'

Melanie sniffs, wipes her face. 'I wish that was enough,' she says and she means this because she does wish there was something he could say that would allow her to open her heart completely, to perform the action of forgiveness.

'How can it be? Your brother is gone.'

It is all too much. She wants to put down the phone but she also wants to keep speaking to him as she waits for some words to soothe her. 'Let's... let's talk about something else, just for a minute.'

'Yes, right, um... Are you doing anything special for New Year's Eve?'

'No, I don't have a boyfriend or anything. I may just have dinner with a few friends. Sorry, I didn't ask about your Christmas.'

'You're... you know, I can picture you; I mean how you looked eight years ago but I can picture you now, a little older but still the same kind person you were. I can hear how kind you are.'

The words surprise her. She has never thought of herself this way because for the last nine years she's had a simmering resentment inside her, a desire to hurt someone who hurt her and every time she has thought of herself, it has been this resentment that is at the forefront of her feelings about herself. 'How do you know I'm kind?'

'Only a kind person would have taken my call. Only a kind person would still be talking to me. It's in your voice, even when you're angry. Only a kind person would ask about my Christmas.'

'That's a nice thing to say,' she says softly, again troubled by the juxtaposition of murderer and ordinary man. 'So did they do anything different for Christmas? I mean I suppose not...'

'They do a nice lunch, turkey and stuff, but no services

because there are a lot of different faiths in here. I did get a card from my mum so that was... good.'

'She didn't visit?'

'No visits are allowed on Christmas Day. She comes once a year, in March, because she lives in Queensland.'

'What is it like when you see her?'

'I don't know... I mean, I'm in here... so. There are a lot of issues to resolve with her but I'm grateful she comes at all.'

'Did I see her at the trial, was she there?'

'No. She's divorced but at the time she was married for the third time. Her husband didn't want her to come. He was a controlling arsehole... sorry, didn't mean to swear.'

She wants to laugh at the incongruity of that statement considering where he is. 'And your dad?'

'Yeah, my dad is definitely not in the picture. And there go the beeps. Can I call you next week?'

'Yes,' she says firmly and she means it.

'Happy New Year, Melanie.'

'Happy New Year,' she replies but she knows he hasn't heard. He's gone. His time on the phone over and for a moment she lets true sympathy for him wash over her. He did a terrible thing but from all accounts, it was the only truly bad thing he had ever done. Can she forgive him? Can she look at his life before the accident and see that he had been trying to make a life for himself? He had not set out to kill her brother. It's not an excuse but perhaps he has paid for the crime. Perhaps he does deserve the second chance she thinks most people deserve. Perhaps.

# TWENTY-THREE

## MELANIE

Sunday, 7 January

In her apartment she is waiting for his call. She refused an invitation to lunch with friends in order to be able to take it. His parole hearing will be soon and she knows that this may be the last chance she has to speak with him. But also, she wants to speak with him. The more they talk, the more curious she has become about his life, about who he is now.

She picks up quickly when the call comes, almost cannot wait to tell the automated voice, 'Yes'. 'Hello.'

'Melanie, Hi.'

'Hi, how are you?'

'Okay, I'm okay, what about you?'

'I'm good, back at work, but good.' The conversation is so casual. No one listening would believe it was between an inmate and a family member of his victim. Melanie finds it strange how easily the extraordinary simply becomes ordinary.

'What do you do?' he asks.

She almost tells him but something stops her. 'Um... is it okay if I don't say...'

'Of course, of course. I get it. Don't worry. I get it.' She has hurt his feelings. It's obvious in his tone.

'It's just that—'

'You don't have to explain. Why don't you tell me what Matthew wanted to do. Is that okay?'

She is transported back to a dinner the night before Matty's grades for his final year of school became available. He needed a high score to get into his chosen university course and Melanie remembers the whole family feeling on edge in case he didn't get the result he needed. They were eating ice cream with chocolate sauce and there was only one scoop left in the tub. She and Matty reached for it at the same time and he quickly sat back, leaving it for her. 'Let's split it,' she said and she can remember thinking that there was no one on earth who deserved to have his dream realised more than her big brother. He got the results he was aiming for, got into the course he wanted but never got to enjoy the career he worked so hard for. Grief, always waiting grief, washes over Melanie and she has to clear her throat to speak.

'Matty wanted to be a vet. God, I haven't thought about that for such a long time. He was so clever, topped all his classes and everyone told him he should go into medicine but he was obsessed with animals. After he died, I didn't think our dog, Milo, would survive. He just lay on his bed all day long, didn't want to go for walks or anything. He was old and he was a family dog but mostly he was Matty's dog.' Milo was a mixed breed dog with beautiful brown eyes and chocolate and cream fur, who always seemed to know which member of the family needed some comfort, often seeking out someone having a bad day and demanding attention. But most of his attention was reserved for Matty who was his best friend.

'That's... poor creature, that's just...'

His distress over the dog is obvious, tears in his voice as he chokes out the words.

'Oh my God, I'm sorry. I didn't mean to make you cry. It's okay, Milo had me and Mum and... he was fine after a bit. I took him to the cemetery to visit Matty's grave and I explained it to him and he seemed to understand. He kind of attached himself to me after that, slept on my bed and followed me around. I probably spoiled him with too many treats. Did you have a dog growing up?'

'Sorry.' He sniffs and coughs. 'I love dogs and I hate to think of one pining for his owner. I didn't have a dog as a kid. My childhood was... well, you kind of already heard some of it at the trial. My mum loved, loves me in her own way but it's complicated. My dad was not good for her and I think she's never really recovered from being with him. And then there was husband number two and three. She could barely take care of herself and her kid. I think a dog would have been one step too far.' His regret over this is obvious and her heart goes out to him.

'Every kid should have a dog. I'm sorry you didn't get to.'

'I'm not telling you this so you should feel sorry for me. I feel like I should explain that. I made my choices the night your brother died and even if I had a shitty childhood, I made the choice to get into the car.'

'You did. But you're still a person.'

'See, you're just so kind. When I talk to you, I feel like myself, like me. It's hard to feel like a person in here. I'm a number, a problem, but somehow speaking to you lets me forget that for a bit.'

Guilt stabs at her. This is how she had been determined to think of him, as a number. And she has tried to do that but somehow his humanness has broken through. He is waiting for something from her and finally, today, she is not resentful about giving it to him. 'Look, I should tell you... I was contacted by the victims' register.'

'Oh, right, yeah, I thought it would be soon.' His relief at her bringing it up is obvious. 'My parole hearing is in a week.'

'They asked if I wanted to do a submission to the State Parole authority about you. I said I would think about it.' And she is thinking about it. She seesaws back and forth but today she feels like she might want to... not exactly help him, but not hinder him at least.

'Okay... thank you for thinking about it.'

'Yeah well, I am, I am thinking about it, I mean. The woman who called told me I had a right, as a victim of your crime, to know what you had done to rehabilitate yourself. I know you joined the bible group and that's good, I guess. But...'

'But you don't know if I've done anything else.'

'Yes.'

'I've served my time and I have tried to use the time well. I left high school at fifteen because I was just a messed-up kid but I have gone back to class in here. I have my HSC now. And I have a trade. I'm a cook.'

'You've become a chef in prison?' she asks, surprised.

His laugh is warm and deep and she realises that it's the first time she's heard him laugh, not that she expected to hear him laugh at all. It brings back the memory of the first time she laughed after Matty died. It was at a video of a puppy falling asleep in his water dish, something silly and simple but she remembers understanding that it was the first time in months she had actually laughed. The action felt strange and then it felt very wrong. She wants to hate this man for his laughter over anything at all but finds she cannot. The conversations have changed something. She no longer has the ease of hating him; instead she must work to maintain her rage at him.

'That's funny. I wouldn't say "chef". More like someone who can get a job in a café or something like that. I work in the kitchens and I'm surprised that I really love it. I don't mind the chopping of all the vegetables, just the boring stuff. I like using my hands.'

'What's your favourite thing to make?'

'Well, this is prison so the food is not exactly gourmet, but I like making cakes. They get us to make cakes for the staff, not the prisoners. I like doing that. If I get to leave, then I'll try and get a job in a café, just something small.'

'You wouldn't think of doing what you were doing before the... before?'

'No. Never. Never, ever... God those beeps.'

She doesn't want the conversation to end. There is more to say, more questions to be answered. 'Look, I'll... make my submission,' she says quickly. 'I'll write something but when you get out... if you get out, I would like to meet. I feel like I need to talk to you without worrying about the conversation being recorded or interrupted.'

'You just tell me where and when and I'll be there. I'll have a parole officer and you can contact him or her and they will know how to contact me. I won't call you. I'll leave it to you to decide if you want to meet me or not. And thank you, Melanie, thank you for speaking to me.'

'I'll make contact,' she says but he's gone.

She knows what she's going to say now, what she's going to write, and when he gets out, she knows what she's going to do then.

# TWENTY-FOUR

## MELANIE

Sunday, 28 January

'Melanie?' She looks around, expecting to see one kind of man but her eyes alight on someone totally different. She smiles to conceal her shock at his appearance. The café is filled with people, all chatting over morning coffee, the smell of roasting beans in the warm summer air.

'Yes, hi, hi.'

'Oh, don't stand up,' he says and then he glances around him, seemingly unsure about what to do. 'Did you order a coffee already? Do I have to go to the counter? Does the waitress come to you?' He sounds panicked at the many possibilities of how to order coffee in a coffee shop and her stomach churns at his anxiety. He is dressed in black jeans and a pale-blue T-shirt but he looks out of place here, not just because of his size and his shaved head, but because he is so uncomfortable.

'Slow down, slow down,' she says softly. 'I ordered. Just go up to the counter and tell them what you want. And tell them table nine,' she says, pointing to the plastic number holder she has on the table.

'Okay, thanks, I'll be back in a sec... just a sec.'

'Take your time.'

He nods gratefully, and makes his way to the counter. A few people glance at him and she wonders if they can tell, if they can see that he's been in prison. She watches him study the menu board. He has not been gone so long that things are so very different but perhaps it is him who is so very different.

While she waits for him to return, she thinks about the words she wrote in her submission to the parole board on his behalf.

*I believe that Mr Elias has used the last eight years to become a better person. I am satisfied that he has paid for his crime. Nothing will bring my brother Matthew back; nothing will change what happened that night. But I believe that Mr Elias is aware of what he did to my family, of how he injured us. Keeping him in prison serves no purpose. I think he wants to get on with his life and I believe that he should be allowed to do this.*

'Right, that's done. I'm not an idiot, I promise, it's just that it feels like I'm in a whole new world. I was only in for eight years but it feels like everything's changed,' he says, coming to sit down opposite her.

'It's okay. I don't think you're an idiot. Not at all. How are you settling in?' She can't stop looking at him, particularly the crooked, obviously broken and badly repaired nose, feeling prickles run along her skin as she imagines the pain it must have caused, imagines the fear he must have felt when he was attacked.

'It's okay. I have a parole officer and I see him once a week at the moment. He helped me get set up with a phone and I've been for a couple of job interviews already in cafés. I think one guy really liked me because he did a stint in jail when he was younger and we just... clicked, I guess.' There is something in his blue eyes as he speaks, a lightness, a joy that comes from this small thing, this very small thing. All around them are people drinking coffee and probably many of them are complaining about everyday things, about work and family and responsibilities and yet this man is excited to just get a job, just get a chance to start over.

'You look different to how I thought you would,' she says as the waitress puts his coffee down in front of him and takes the number from the table. 'I mean you've changed.'

'Yeah, it's the weights. I joined a gym near my house because I think it's good to keep going. I was just a skinny kid when I went inside. And, of course, my nose has been broken a couple of times.' He touches his face self-consciously and her heart goes out to him.

After the accident, when they learned he had been arrested and then in the court proceedings that followed, she had hated him with a depth of intensity she never believed possible. She had wished him dead, wished his family dead, wished hell and damnation on him and everyone he loved because Matty, lovely Matty who was studying to be a vet, was gone. She never thought time would heal her wound, especially after her mother got sick, but it has done some of the job. What surprised Melanie is how talking to this man has helped. He is a human being again, someone who has paid a terrible price for being in a car that caused a death.

And she has come unstuck. That's what she wanted, what she hoped for from speaking with him, that she would be able to move forward, not in two parallel lines with her nineteen-year-old self, but as a whole. She feels like she can now, like they have blended into one person who still mourns her brother but is also able to accept that it's okay for her to have her own happiness. A monster didn't rear up out of the darkness and kill her brother but rather a man who made a mistake.

'Did it... did it hurt?' she asks hesitantly, lifting her finger to touch her own nose.

'Like you wouldn't believe,' he says and then he takes a sip of his coffee. 'I don't remember coffee tasting this good.'

'Maybe you're just so used to prison coffee.' She smiles.

'Maybe,' he agrees.

'So, listen...' She stops speaking, wondering if this is the right thing to do. Right now, she has so many questions.

Throughout their calls she has known that there was something else he wanted to say, something else he wanted to tell her but couldn't. In court he had answered his lawyer's questions in a monotone, looked down rather than at people, sometimes giving his head a shake.

He had been especially distraught when his boss at the time of the accident testified against him, rubbing his face frequently and slumping low in his chair whenever the man spoke.

When his boss testified to his drinking on the job, he had turned scarlet, his head shaking 'no' as Melanie watched him clench his fists. It is only since her conversations with him that she has begun to think about the trial in a different way, that she wonders if something else happened that night and he was prevented from discussing it, perhaps by his own lawyer. She has no idea why she believes this is the case but she cannot get the thought out of her mind.

'So, I wanted you to tell me the story, the whole story, from the beginning. I told the parole board that I thought you'd served your sentence and that's the truth.'

'Thank you for that. I don't know if thank you is enough but it's all I've got right now.'

'It's fine. I just want the whole story. I feel like there's more to it. I heard it all at the trial and you told it to me again on the phone but...'

He nods and then he looks around the café, lacing his fingers together and cracking his knuckles.

'There is more,' he says without looking at her.

'There is?' she asks and then she waits for him to look at her and when he does, he just nods.

'Can you...' She finds the words stuck in her throat and leans down, picks up her coffee and takes too big a sip, burning her throat. She coughs.

'You okay?' he asks, leaning towards her and raising his hand as if to pat her on the back but immediately lowering it again. Melanie nods and then she takes a breath.

'I want to know everything,' she says. 'I want to know exactly what happened that night.'

'I should not have been in a car. I was very drunk,' he says, 'but...'

'But?'

'But I wasn't driving, Melanie. I wasn't driving my car.'

The sound of chatter in the café fades as Melanie holds her body so still, she can hear herself breathing.

'But...' she begins and then she cannot think of how to ask the questions, of what to say.

'I told the police and my lawyer the truth. I told everyone I could the truth but I had no way to prove it. Eventually they told me, I mean my lawyer advised me, that it would go very badly for me at trial if I stuck to that story. There was no evidence of anyone else at the scene, no way to prove anyone else was there. They told me I would be sentenced for the maximum if I said someone else was driving, especially since he denied it from day one and there was no way to prove it, no way at all.'

'Who?' she says, because it's the only thing she needs to know.

'My boss.'

'The guy who testified against you, who said you drank at work?'

'Yes, he was driving.'

'He was driving?' she says, unsure if she has heard right.

'We had dinner together at the bar and we drank together and when we left, he was the one driving and no one believed me.'

'But surely people saw you together at the bar and leaving the bar?'

'They did see us together but no one saw us getting into my car. I had no actual proof and he was a respected man in the community, a family man, and I was a kid who had never managed to stay in school. I was awkward, not good at making myself clear, lost... I was someone it was easy to disbelieve. And they simply didn't believe me. Not the police and not my lawyer, no one.'

She can feel that later, she will be angry; when she's had time to think about this, rage and fury will rise inside her but right now all she has is incomprehension.

'You're going to need to explain it to me,' she says.

'Okay, whew,' he says, rubbing his shaved head with his hand. 'The night of the accident, I went out to dinner with my boss, you remember that, right?'

'I do, he said that he didn't want to go to dinner with you, but he ended up going anyway.'

'Yeah, but he lied. He was the one who invited me to dinner. Well, actually told me we had to go to dinner to celebrate a big sale.'

'So you were at dinner together at a pub and... what?'

'We were drinking.'

'I know and he said that he told you to slow down on the drinking.' She remembers the trial. She remembers the man's words.

'He lied. He never said that.'

'But...' she says, confused again, and he sits forward, links his hands.

'He was the one buying the drinks, Melanie. I was only nineteen. I wasn't exactly earning a lot of money and what I was earning, I was using to support myself and my grandmother. I would have stopped drinking the moment he stopped buying but he kept buying and he was my boss. I wasn't exactly in a position to say no. I had only been in the job a few months. I just wanted to stay employed. I screwed up at school, like I told you, and I thought I had found a job that would let me make something of myself.'

'I get it. I've been the newbie. I know how hard it is but no one was forcing you.' She stares down into her coffee cup, not wanting to see that truth hit him.

'No, you're right about that,' he replies softly.

She looks up at him again. 'When your boss said that he told you, at the end of the night, that you were not fit to drive... he lied?'

'It was actually the other way around. I suggested walking or getting a cab. I said there was no way I was going to drive.'

'Then why did you get in your car? Why did you drive?'

'That's the whole point, that's what I kept trying to tell the police and my lawyer and no one would listen. I wasn't driving. It was my car but I wasn't driving.'

'But your boss said that he walked back to the office, that he wasn't in the car with you...?'

'That was the biggest lie of all.'

Melanie takes a deep breath. She has forgotten the name of the man who was his boss. Many people had testified at the trial but she had only held on to the most important name, the name of the man who killed Matthew.

Peter Elias. That was the only name she had needed to remember.

'What's his name?' she asks and Peter's eyes darken for a moment. Melanie feels that she has somehow betrayed him by not remembering but then she had no idea.

'Leo Palmer.' Peter spits out the name, the pain he feels in saying it is obvious.

'I need to hear the whole story, okay? I need to hear it,' she says.

'You do,' he agrees and he picks up his cup of coffee and then he sits back in his chair.

And he begins to speak and as she listens, she understands that she will not be the same after this, that the wound of her brother's death has been reopened and she will have no real idea how to sew it closed again. Nineteen-year-old Melanie is back, filled with anguish and despair, rage and anger.

# TWENTY-FIVE

## MELANIE

Sunday, 26 February

Melanie glances at the clock on her dashboard, worried that she will be late to meet Peter for lunch. A new patient was transferred into her care home today from somewhere else, Mr Sharma. His daughter lives overseas and was worried that he wasn't receiving proper care and she was right. The man was malnourished and confused and Melanie needed to take some extra time with him to get him settled. He was so grateful to be cared for that it made Melanie want to cry.

The care home is twenty minutes away from the café and in order to make up time she turned off a busy road but now she's lost. She should have just used Google Maps. She pulls over and keys in the address of the café and then gets back on the road. Peter worries if she's late. He doesn't say it but despite the time they have already spent together, he is always worried that she will never show up again, never want to speak to him again.

'You believe me, don't you?' he has asked her over and again, unsure if she is as filled with doubt as the police and his lawyer were nine years ago.

Melanie has gone back and forth on this, although she has always just said, 'yes' when Peter asks.

Why would he lie now? What purpose would it serve? He cannot get his years back and Leo Palmer will never have to pay for what he did, so why lie?

She stops at a traffic light and watches a whole lot of people cross in front of her car. She is admiring a blue dress worn by a young woman crossing when a man catches her eye and her heart jumps.

Leo Palmer.

She has only seen him in real life once before, in court so many years ago now, but she googled him after Peter told her the whole story, stalked him on Instagram and every other profile he has, read about him on the internet, saw how many sales he made last year for his real estate agency. Looked at his professional photo on the estate agency website, that trust-me-I'm-an-estate-agent smile, and every time she looked, she was filled with that rage, again and again.

He ambles across the road, his head tilted to one side as he speaks into his phone, a large coffee in one hand. Her window is slightly open and she hears the words, 'you know me, I'm always the lucky one.' It's so clearly him, as though he is the walking photograph from the agency in an expensive blue suit that moves with his body, broad shoulders and perfectly styled brown hair.

The shock of seeing him in an unexpected place steals the air in her lungs and she coughs.

He walks slowly as he talks and then, suddenly, he is in front of her car and he abruptly laughs. 'It's all good, really good,' he says. He turns his head for a moment, seeing her but not seeing her and then he looks ahead again.

Her foot begins to lift off the brake as she allows herself to explore the image of her car slamming into his body, his head rocking back, the coffee falling to the ground, the phone bouncing and cracking on the street.

The light turns green and she moves her foot to the accelerator, not giving herself a chance to think about it but as she moves, he steps nimbly onto the sidewalk, another laugh piercing through the air.

She moves through the intersection, risking a quick look back but he is already gone, around a corner and away from her. Her heart is racing at what she wanted to do.

'I could have killed him,' she thinks. *I should have killed him.*

In the café she finds a table, sits down, her emotions all over the place. She is here on time but Peter is running late. Should she tell him? She can't tell him.

'Hey, Mel, sorry I'm late, Joe was going through the new dessert menu with me.' Peter touches her lightly on the back and she smiles. She won't say anything. Peter doesn't need to hear that the man who he went to prison for is out in the world, living his best life. She'll keep that pain for herself.

'Don't worry. I was quite happy sitting here. It's so hot outside.' The air conditioning in the café has been turned up high. She's shivering but it's not from the air conditioning.

'I know, it doesn't seem like autumn is just around the corner. I feel like something savoury. I've never tasted so many sweet things at once,' says Peter and Melanie laughs, trying to dismiss Leo Palmer from her mind.

Peter is working more hours than he's being paid for because he loves the work. But today he looks more tired than usual, as his eyes dart from side to side in the café, as though he is searching for someone.

'Is Joe happy with your suggestions, with the stuff you made?' she asks.

Peter looks at her and she can see him making an effort to concentrate. 'He loves the cronut made with chocolate and raspberry and the one made with chocolate and caramel but he's not sure about the one with the mint cream.'

'Ah, I loved that one.' In her small kitchen, he had mixed up the ingredients for all his dessert ideas, talking about what made each one different, letting her taste everything along the way until she got to enjoy the final product.

'That's because you love anything with mint.' He smiles but she can see something is bothering him.

'You know I do.' They share a glance and then he looks away. Something is wrong. He's doing so well but he is under strict parole conditions. He has to meet with his parole officer once a week and he's not allowed to drink alcohol for the next four months until he has been discharged although that's not a problem for him. 'I don't know how I will ever take a drink again,' he has told her.

'Have you looked at the menu?' he asks, his eyes moving over the laminated page.

Melanie picks up the menu, shaking her head. 'I'll have...' she reads through the choices, not hungry but not wanting Peter to ask her why, 'the Caesar salad with chicken.'

'Great, I'll have that too.' He puts the menu down and again, looks around the café as though he thinks someone may be watching him.

'Right, ordering on the app,' she says, opening up her phone and scanning the small circle with an app on their table, 'and... done.' She relaxes in her chair and waits. Peter cracks his knuckles, smiles distractedly at her. Melanie doesn't ask. He'll tell her if he wants her to know.

'There's something we need to discuss,' he says finally. He rests his hands on his legs, jiggles his knees up and down.

'You sound so serious; what do we need to discuss?' They have been meeting every week since he was released and speaking on the phone often. It feels natural, like a friendship that just evolved. If she thinks too long about being friends with the man who went to prison for her brother's death, she gets anxious about getting to know him but then she sees him or speaks to him and it seems impossible that she will not speak to him again. She is used to the way he looks now, used to the shaved head and the muscled arms. He is no longer scary; he is just Peter. And, of course, she knows the truth.

'Peter,' she says softly because he seems to be struggling to find the words.

'He came into the café yesterday.' The words are spoken slowly, heavy with despair.

'Who?'

'Leo. Leo Palmer came into my café.' A gut punch of a phrase. Here Leo Palmer is – twice in one day. *What are the chances?*

'Oh... oh God... what did you do?' she asks Peter who has fallen silent.

'Nothing,' he says, and then he rubs his hand over his head where he keeps his dark hair shaved short. 'I actually served him because one waitress was out sick and Joe asked me to help serve. He ordered a coffee and the breakfast sandwich.'

'And you served him, you actually took his order?' It's not hard to see what this must have done to Peter and she steels herself for the story of the confrontation that must have occurred. Peter doesn't have a temper but prison taught him how to access his aggression to save himself. And how could you not confront the man who ruined your life?

'I didn't take it, Jessa did, but then she was slammed so I was delivering the orders to tables in between making stuff and I took him his sandwich and his coffee.'

'And what... what happened?' Her heart is in her throat as she studies him. He doesn't say anything for a minute, his eyes darting around the café again, and then the waitress puts their salads down in front of them, places cutlery and leaves with a smile. Neither of them moves.

'Nothing.' He meets her gaze as his blue eyes shine with tears.

'I don't understand.'

'Absolutely nothing,' he says, shaking his head in disbelief. 'He looked up at me when I put the food down in front of him and said, "Thanks, mate." I just stood there and then I asked him if he needed anything else, just so he would look at me and he did, he looked right at me and then he shook his head and looked back down at his phone. And I just stood there like some kind of loser until he said, "I don't need anything else." I could tell he was irritated that I was still there but that's all he was, irritated. I... I felt like the world was kind of tilting. I got dizzy and I felt sick. And I went back into the kitchen and I sat down on the floor until Joe came to find me and he didn't even yell at me. He just said, "Tell me what you need," and I asked if I could have half an hour.

'I went outside and I watched him through the window of the café until he got up to leave and then I followed him for a block and the whole time I was doing that, I wanted to run up to him and tell him to see me, to recognise me, but I was too scared. I was too weak and too stupid and...' Peter rocks backwards and forwards in his chair, his chest heaving as he takes deep breaths.

'Hey, hey, it's okay, it's okay. Calm down,' Melanie says, reaching out and touching him on the shoulder.

'Sorry, I'm okay. After a few minutes I realised what I was doing and I turned back and then I just stopped thinking about it. I did my work and I got through the day and now... I don't know that I can just let this go, Mel. I can't just have this guy walking around free to do as he pleases after what he did to my life, after what he did to your brother.' He picks up his knife and fork as if to begin eating but immediately replaces them on the table, his appetite also, obviously gone.

'Okay... it's okay. I understand. I do.'

'You do?'

'I do. Because I saw him, I just saw him. I was on my way here and there he was, in the street. I saw him.'

'God, what did you do?'

'I...' She shakes her head. Can she confess her murderous thoughts to him? What will he think of her?

'I thought about killing him, about just driving through the intersection and killing him,' she says, as her hands twist the paper serviette she is holding.

'Oh Mel,' he says, leaning forward and covering her hands with one of his own.

'You're right, he shouldn't be allowed to just get away with it, to just go on living his life like he never did anything,' she says.

'But he will, there's nothing we can do,' says Peter.

Melanie nods, understanding.

'Can we go to the police? Can we tell them your story again?'

'They didn't believe me then. Why would they believe me now? And there's my parole. If it looks like I'm trying to say I never committed the crime in the first place...'

Melanie doesn't know what to say to that.

'I wish there was a way to get him to tell the truth. If he told the truth...'

'He'll never do that, Peter. He has a family, a job, a life. He wouldn't ever do that.'

'Not unless he wasn't given a choice,' agrees Peter and he picks up his knife and fork, starts eating and for the first time in a while, Melanie is afraid of Peter and what he might do.

'Maybe he's changed,' she says, hopeful that this might be possible. 'Maybe after he got away with it, he's been consumed by guilt? He could be a very different man to who he was nine years ago.'

'No,' says Peter. 'When I worked for him, he was... not a

good person. And I reached out to him when I was in prison, I did. I tried to get him to… I tried.' He puts a forkful of the salad in his mouth and chews while Melanie waits for him to explain.

'Why did he do it?' Melanie asks him. 'Why do you think he did it? And how could he have done it? How?'

'He made a decision on the night,' says Peter. 'He decided that his life was worth more than mine.'

Melanie nods, understanding.

'And he really shouldn't have been allowed to get away with that. Not then and not now either.'

'I agree,' says Melanie. She picks up her cutlery and eats some of her salad as she and Peter sit in silence.

'So how do we make sure that doesn't happen?' she says finally.

Peter stops eating and looks at her. His shoulders go back and it's like something changes in the air, a silent agreement being made between the two of them. They will not accept that there is 'nothing they can do'.

Because maybe, just maybe, there is something that can be done.

'How do we make sure he pays for what he's done?' she asks, giving the words air, giving Peter permission to think this way, giving herself permission to think this way.

'I don't know yet,' says Peter. 'But I won't be able to do anything else with my life until I figure that out.'

'I'm here for you, whatever you want to do. I'm here for you,' she says.

'I know.' He nods his head. 'I know.'

# PART THREE

NOW

# TWENTY-SIX

## LEO

Last Night

It's 10 p.m. on Saturday night and Leo is in his car, with an envelope filled with cash. A situation that is so unbelievable, it's almost laughable.

He's been played by a pro. Hopefully, once this is done, Serena or whoever the hell she is will find herself another sucker.

> *Meet me at Barton Park. 10.15 p.m. Don't be late, lover boy.*
> *I'll be by the climbing frame.*

The text came through this afternoon, making him sick at the idea that they would be meeting at a park where his kids had played when they were little. He should never have given in to the temptation to continue this affair in Sydney. Sleeping with someone at a conference was one thing, bringing it home was another. He'd always been so careful about separating his life in Sydney from the moments of unreality offered by the conferences. But he had been lured into Serena's web, a willingly stupid fly.

And after midnight, he is meeting Peter Denton. He doesn't have any cash for Peter Denton, but he does have his tyre iron. Let the man see what he's made of. Leo is betting that even the slightest amount of physical aggression will cower him. And then this too will be over.

As he drives, his meeting earlier today with Martin circles in his head.

It had only been hours ago. Saturdays were busy days in real estate but Martin had insisted on getting together and Leo had no choice but to agree. He wanted to get it over with anyway. Leo hadn't eaten breakfast, his stomach churning all morning as he tried to figure a way through the maze of his problems. Serena Burns and Peter Denton – two tormentors who needed to be obliterated.

He had been unable to sit still in the meeting with Martin, cracking his knuckles and fixing his tie constantly.

'So, this is an unfortunate situation, isn't it?' Martin said in his usual measured way as soon as Leo was seated in his office. Martin Gantry started his agency thirty years ago and has grown it to become one of the biggest single agencies in Sydney, refusing to sell out and become part of one of the chains. He is a good-looking man in his late sixties with his eyes on retirement. No one knows who's going to take over for Martin when he does finally decide that he's had enough but Leo always imagined that it might be him, has been pinning his hopes on that fact. Right now that seems an impossibility but once this is all sorted, he may just be back on track.

Martin liked him and, in the past, Leo has been one of the best performing salesmen in the office. Martin wouldn't want to get rid of a top performer even if he was currently struggling.

'I am going to sort it out, Martin, I can promise you that. I have a meeting arranged with the man, and I will be making every effort to make sure he's happy.' He didn't have anything arranged at the time and he didn't care if Peter Denton was happy or not, only that he went away.

'And how will you do that, Leo? Why did you not let this woman back out of the sale? Why would you have pushed her into it in the first place? You know that elderly clients sometimes need someone to help them navigate something like this. I understand she told you that her grandson asked her to wait.'

'Who told you that?' snapped Leo and then he shook his head to apologise for the outburst.

'Blake,' said Martin. 'She heard it from Robbie and they were both concerned. How are you planning to make this go away? Do you think you've done the right thing here? Is the agency going to suffer for this?'

Martin fired his questions at Leo. Leo's stomach bubbled and churned. He had held up his hands to get Martin to give him a chance to talk.

'I promise you that I gave her every opportunity to back out. She was the one who said she didn't want a cooling-off period. She was the one who really wanted the sale to go ahead. I think that what we have here is a case of a grandson being upset about his inheritance. He was probably hoping that she lived in the house until she died and then he would get the money from the sale and now that money will be spent on something else and between stamp duty and lawyer's fees, some of that inheritance will be whittled away. He's angry about that. He doesn't care about his grandmother.'

'Um hmm,' Martin said as he spoke, nodding his head. 'But if this is the case, why have you not responded to his emails? Why have you not engaged a lawyer? Why have you let this situation get so out of control?'

'I've been speaking to her and she's assured me that she is speaking to her grandson. I didn't want to get in the middle of a family issue.' He made sure to maintain eye contact. Dropping eye contact when you're lying is a dead giveaway.

Martin had nodded his head again. 'Right, but now you will be speaking directly to him and you will get this sorted out?'

'Absolutely, by tomorrow, this will all be over.' Leo stood up as he hoped and prayed that would be the case. In his pocket his phone was on vibrate as he waited for Serena's text on where and when she wanted her money.

'Right, get it done and let me know when I can tell our lawyers to stand down,' Martin said, and Leo nodded gratefully, leaving and going back to his office where he closed the door and slid down onto the floor so that people outside looking through the window of the agency couldn't see him. His heart was racing and he wanted to be sick. So many lies. He knew he would need to brief Robbie about what to say to Martin if he was asked. Robbie should not have said anything to Blake and what does Blake have against him? He's indulged in some mild flirting with her but she seems keen on Robbie. Everyone flirts with her, he's sure. She's young and pretty. What does she expect?

Leo dropped his head into his hands, massaging his temples to get rid of his ever-present headache.

And then the text came in from Serena, detailing where to meet.

Leo had stared down at the words, remaining on the floor. And then he had emailed Peter Denton.

Meet me at midnight tonight. Barton Park. He added the address so the man would know where it was.

Fine, came the immediate reply, which had surprised Leo.

He and Serena would be done by then. Hopefully it was just her and she took the cash and he never saw her again. Unless this was just the beginning. Please God, let it not be just the beginning. He doesn't want to contemplate what happens if she's brought her psycho boyfriend with her. But he has the tyre iron just in case.

This afternoon, Leo had no idea what he was actually going to do about Peter Denton. But now that he's driving, the tyre iron next to him on the passenger seat, he can see that he may have to defend himself against the man. A whole story has unfolded in his mind of how it will go down.

Peter Denton had agreed to meet him at midnight. Why? No one brings their lawyer to a meeting at midnight. When Leo organised this, he had expected the man to tell him 'No' but instead he had agreed. He means to do Leo harm, that's for sure, and that means Leo has no choice but to defend himself. And that's what he's going to do. He can just imagine explaining this to the police. What he's hoping for is that Peter Denton can be talked around. Leo will cite the law, will let him know his grandmother made her own choices and that she didn't want Leo to talk to him. The woman is in her eighties and her grandson hasn't seen her for some time – who knows how long. Leo can hint that she may have undiagnosed dementia, which he hadn't picked up on. The argument, the persuasive words he will use, the explanations he will offer, go around in his head. If all else fails, he has his tyre iron.

Despite where he is and what he's going to do, after days of feeling hopeless about his life, Leo is feeling just a little more upbeat than he has been. His car will go in to get repaired, the smell, which he is pretty sure is a dead rat stuck somewhere inside the engine block, will be removed. An old saying, 'love rat', crosses his mind. Of course it's a rat, no points for subtlety from Serena or the boyfriend. Leo shakes his head. Whatever it is, this whole thing will be over soon.

Serena will go away and Peter Denton will accept his grandmother has sold her house and move on with his life, or he won't and Leo will have to think of something else. But it feels like he's on his way to put this whole horrible time behind him.

And he's made a decision. He will reinvent himself, change who Leo Palmer is. Once this is over, he's going to do better at life. He's going to be a better husband and father and even a better real estate agent. He's going to be the kind of man people talk about as being just an all-around good guy. No more affairs, no more lying, no more anything except just being grateful for what he has. What he cannot lose. At home, his twin sons are tucked up in bed and Diana is watching some cooking show on television. 'Just meeting some guys for a drink,' he told her an hour ago. She had raised her eyebrows in a question. It was late to go out but he didn't give her the chance to ask him which friends he was meeting.

He stops at an orange light and sits on the quiet street, his knee jiggling up and down as he waits through the red and then when it turns green, he pulls off, carefully looking both ways. He's new Leo now. Leo the careful driver, Leo the good husband and father, Leo the honest real estate agent. That's who he is now.

# TWENTY-SEVEN

## MELANIE

She is Serena again. Casually dressed but wearing all the make-up, the contact lenses and the wig as she stands near the climbing frame in the park. Her coat is wrapped tightly around her as the wind whistles through the trees. Her whole body trembles with cold or fear or both.

What if he doesn't come?

What if he does?

She turns to look behind her to a section of the park thick with bushes and trees. She wishes this were over.

The headlights of a car appear, the car driving right up to the small parking lot near the children's playground and stopping. Melanie's heart thrums inside her. The swings in the playground move back and forth, their steel chains jangling in the wind.

A car door opens and Leo climbs out. He is dressed warmly in a jacket and carrying a tyre iron. Melanie takes a step back as he walks towards her. She looks behind at the trees and bushes.

'Serena,' says Leo, his eyes narrowed and cold.

'Leo,' she says. Why is he carrying a tyre iron?

'Is your boyfriend here?' he asks.

'Do you have the money?' she replies.

Leo nods, takes an envelope out of his jacket and throws it in her direction where it drops onto the floor, notes spilling out of the envelope, one of them skittering along the playground matting in the wind.

Melanie doesn't move. She's not going to get down on her knees in front of him.

'I want you to know something,' she says.

'That you're a scam artist working with the man who damaged my car and my office? I know that.'

Melanie doesn't say anything. Leo is on edge, jittery with anger. He's not going to give her what she wants, she can feel it. But she needs to try.

'Don't you want to know why?' she asks.

'Because it's just what you do, I imagine,' he sneers. 'You're a con artist, a criminal, you belong in jail.'

'Leo, do you remember a car accident nine years ago?' she asks quickly.

'What?' he says.

'Nine years ago, there was a car accident. A young man was killed.'

Leo stares at her for a moment and at first there is confusion on his face but then she watches him shift, the tyre iron swings once or twice and she can see that he knows what she's talking about.

'I don't understand.'

'But you do, Leo. Nine years ago, there was a car accident and someone died. And someone went to jail. A man named Peter Elias.'

Leo points the tyre iron at her and Melanie takes another step back. He smiles. 'Oh, you are good, you are very good at this. Wow, I'm actually impressed that you took the time to research everything. You've done your homework on my whole life, haven't you? Well done, Serena,' he sneers.

'Finding my name connected with that must have taken some digging.'

'You belong in jail, Leo. You don't deserve anything that you have and you belong in jail for what you did.'

In Melanie's pocket, her phone is recording the conversation. All she needs is him admitting what he did and then they can decide what to do. They just want the confession.

'You are an excellent con artist.' Leo smiles. 'Are you going to tell me you've infected my computer next? Do you have nude pictures of me you're going to share on the internet? I have to admire your commitment to this, Serena.'

She clears her throat. This is not going well but she has to keep trying. 'This is not a con. You belong in jail, Leo. You've gotten away with it for too long.' Her voice is trembling. He isn't taking this seriously. He thinks she's a joke.

Leo walks right up to her and before she can even step back his hands are around her neck.

'You belong in jail,' he says. 'You.' His eyes are dark in the dim light of the park, the wrinkles around his mouth more pronounced in a deep frown.

Melanie waves her hands as she coughs. 'Pl... please,' she coughs, 'you need... to let go... or you'll get... hurt.'

Leo lets go abruptly and looks around the park. 'He's here, isn't he? Your psycho boyfriend.'

Melanie nods, rubbing her neck and struggling to take a deep breath. 'Leo,' she says, 'you've seen what he can do; you know what he's capable of. I need you to tell me the truth about what happened nine years ago. That's all we want, the truth.'

'Who are you?' Leo asks. 'I mean, what's your real name?' He peers at her, studying her face. 'You look... have I met you before? I mean before the conference?' There is no fear in his voice, only curiosity. While he stares at her, he hunches down and picks up the envelope of cash, holds it out to her. 'Take it and get out of my life. I will go to the police if I ever hear from you again.'

'You'll go to the police? And what will your wife say? What will everyone else in your life say? What will your boys think of you, Leo? You'll be the man who broke their mother's heart.'

Leo is silent at that, still watching her. Her heart is pounding but she has to convince him. They are so close. Leo is here to protect his marriage, his family. He doesn't want to have his affair exposed or he wouldn't be here in a playground with an envelope full of cash.

He needs Serena to go away.

Going to the police would shine a spotlight on his cheating and his lies and he doesn't want that.

'I know you lied about the accident nine years ago and the person I'm here with knows it too. I don't want you to get hurt. You need to tell me the truth.'

Leo looks around the park and he takes a step back. 'This is how you do it, isn't it? You want me to say something else so you can go on blackmailing me forever. Even if I was involved in any way in a car accident years ago, and I wasn't, do you actually think I would give you any more ammunition to blackmail me with?' He is holding the envelope of cash and now he puts it back into his jacket. 'I'm actually not falling for any of this crap. You want to tell my wife about us, go ahead. Maybe my marriage is over anyway. You do what you want, Serena. I'm not getting caught in some bullshit cycle of blackmail.'

He turns and starts to walk away. He is calling her bluff. 'Please, Leo,' she calls, 'if you just tell me the truth this can be over. Just talk to me or someone is going to get hurt.'

Leo stops at his car. 'Screw you and him, Serena,' he calls over the whistling wind. 'This has nothing to do with nine years ago. I don't know what you think you know but, trust me, you don't know anything. This is some kind of scam. Don't contact me again or I will go to the police.' He gets into his car and with a screech of his wheels, he's gone.

Melanie drops her head. The wind slices through the playground and she trembles, pulling her coat closer to her body. It hasn't worked. All that time, all those afternoons in hotel rooms and letting him touch her and smiling at him and laughing at his jokes, wearing the wig and dressing up as somebody else. It hasn't worked. She has failed Peter, failed herself and her family.

'Now,' she hears behind her, 'it's my turn.'

She wants to protest but all she can do is nod. She had a plan and it hasn't worked.

But what's coming next is not something she can bear to think about.

# TWENTY-EIGHT

## DIANA

She is lying in bed, on her side, when he comes in. She keeps her eyes closed, pretending to be asleep. He goes into the bathroom and then she hears the shower being turned on.

Has he given them the money and the confession they really want? Is it over now?

'What are you going to do if he confesses?' she had asked the man in the coffee shop, the man who looked nothing like the boy who had been sentenced to ten years in prison for killing someone. She had only met Peter Elias once before the accident and all she can remember of him is a young boy with nice eyes and a desperation to please Leo. When the accident happened, she had not been able to marry the shy young man with the idea of a callous drunk driver who was going to prison. She knows why now.

She hadn't wanted to believe anything he said in the coffee shop but then she came home and finally opened the letters from Long Vale Correctional Facility in Leo's drawer. She didn't even care if he caught her, if he came in and demanded to know what she was doing. She had read through them all, captured by the written words as the boys' voices, raised in an argument over what television show to watch, drifted in through the closed study door.

So many letters from a desperate young man.

*Dear Leo, I'm begging you to tell the truth. You know what happened. Please, I won't survive in here...*

*Dear Leo, I'm asking you to search your heart for some humanity. I'm writing this from the hospital. Last night I was beaten up and I've got four cracked ribs and a broken nose. I've never known that kind of pain...*

*Dear Leo, please, only you can help me. If you confess that you were involved, they'll go easy on you...*

*Dear Leo, please can you reply to one of my letters? You lied about everything. How can you live with yourself?...*

*Dear Leo, what kind of man are you? I've been here for two years now. I will never be the same again. I wasn't driving Leo, you know that...*

*Dear Leo, I will never be able to forgive you for this...*

*Dear Leo, who are you? Who exactly do you think you are?...*

*Dear Leo, I think I can forgive you. I know you were scared as well and I think I can find a way to forgive you...*

There were so many letters. The last one was dated six months ago. It was in the same handwriting but not from prison.

*Dear Leo,*

*I'm free, no thanks to you. You would know I was out if you
looked up from your phone. You would have seen me staring
down at you. And you would know. I thought I had forgiven
you, but I haven't. Watch out for me, Leo. Watch out...*

Shivers ran up and down her spine as she read the words.
Leo didn't want to know. He didn't want to hear what his lies
had done to the young man who used to work for him and so he
never opened a single letter. Not a single one. All that pain, all
that desperation had been callously ignored, gone unnoticed
and unread and unacknowledged by her husband.

He had probably not even registered that the last one didn't
come from a prison. But he kept them instead of throwing them
away. Why? Guilt? Shame? Or something more nefarious?
What did he think he would need them for?

It pains Diana to admit that she has been married to
someone who has gotten further and further away from the
young man she met one night in a bar. But perhaps this Leo, the
cheating, lying Leo, has always been there. She could have just
walked away from all this but he is part of her boys: Rowan,
with his gregarious nature; Sawyer, with his attention to detail.
Leo is in both of them. And if he has given them the confession,
then perhaps he can work towards becoming a better man for
his sons. That's what Diana is hoping for.

When the accident happened, the twins were only six
months old and she was still struggling to get a few hours of
uninterrupted sleep.

The night of the accident, she remembers Leo sliding into
bed late, waking her and irritating her but not much else. She
doesn't remember if he smelled of alcohol.

The next morning, the accident had been on the news. The
tragedy of one drunk nineteen-year-old man killing a twenty-
one-year-old man in a terrible accident was shocking. She
remembers because she had looked at her boys in their high

chairs as she listened to the story and tried to imagine them at an age where they could drive or drink, where they could hurt someone or be hurt themselves and even though she was exhausted, she had been grateful that they were still little, that she was still able to protect them from the whole world.

When it came out that the man driving the car that caused a death had worked for Leo, she had been horrified.

'I always thought there was something odd about him,' Leo told her. 'I caught him drinking on the job once or twice.'

And then he had to be interviewed by the police and he had confessed to her that he had been out with Peter that night, celebrating a big sale, but that he had walked back to the office instead of getting in the car with someone who was drunk.

'But then how did your car get home?' she asked.

'I... slept for an hour at the office and then I realised I was actually quite sober, so I drove home.' Diana had accepted that explanation. Perhaps she had accepted it too easily.

'Why didn't you stop him driving? You're his boss,' she said.

'He told me he was just going to sleep it off in his car. I didn't think he was going to drive,' Leo said, shaking his head sadly.

And she believed him. Not only that, she hadn't pushed or questioned too much as she slogged through her days with the twins.

In the coffee shop, she hadn't wanted to believe Peter but she kept questioning why he would be lying. He had served his time. He was free so why lie now?

'What do you have to do with the woman he's sleeping with?'

'She's a... friend,' he said and Diana understood that there was more to that.

'Why not just confront him?' she asked. 'Why all this cloak and dagger rubbish?'

'Leo thinks nothing can touch him,' Peter said. 'He lied to

the police, to the court, to the world. He thinks he's invincible. He needs to know he's not. And...'

'And?' she asked.

'He didn't have to sleep with her. He doesn't have to do half the shitty things he does but he does them. I thought he may have used the time since the accident to become a better human being. I thought he would be doing penance in his own way, even though he never replied to one of my letters. But he has done nothing but indulge his own selfish needs. He needs to confess.'

Diana's cheeks flamed at the way he was speaking about the man she slept next to every night. *Don't talk about him like that. He's not all bad. You should see him when he does engage with the boys, how quickly he delights them, how much they love him.*

'And then what?' was all she could manage to say to the man sitting opposite her.

Peter shrugged. 'We'll see.'

'I'm not going to help you entrap my husband,' Diana spat.

'He's already done that to himself,' said Peter and then he stood up and walked away before turning around again. 'You can help us get him to a place where he might be desperate enough to tell the truth and then it can end quickly, but otherwise...'

'Okay,' said Diana quickly, hearing the threat. 'Okay.'

'She'll be in touch,' he said and then he was gone.

The picture was meant to scare him, the request for money to put him on edge enough that when he went to the park and he was told that everything they had been doing could get worse, he would tell them what they wanted to know.

Even after Peter had told her his story, Diana wanted to go to the police but each time that thought rolled into her head, she wondered how she would explain why Peter and the woman were doing what they were doing. And how would she state, categorically, to the police, that she believed they were lying about Leo? Leo had lied to her many times in their marriage. He had lied and cheated. What else was he capable of?

The letters told her everything she needed to know.

Leo had driven drunk and killed a man and then let someone else take the blame. And what was worse is that she questioned, if she had known, what would she, as the mother of twin babies, have wanted him to do? If he had gone to jail, it would have devastated her life, changed her life and the boys' lives forever. What would she have done? Would she have said, 'Keep quiet, lie, stay with us, we need you'?

Or would she have said, 'Confess; go to the police and jail?'

She had been drowning in new babies, almost delirious some days from lack of sleep. 'Keep quiet,' she has to admit she would have said. 'I can't do this alone.' And she had felt a hot flush of shame and guilt at her own need for self-preservation. She couldn't judge anyone, had no right to judge anyone.

That's the thing about perspective. There are people in prison for heinous crimes who have regular visits from their loved ones and it's easy to ask: why not just stop seeing them, cut them out of your life, move on? It's easy to ask those questions until you are faced with that possibility yourself. Diana was pretty sure she didn't want to be married to Leo anymore but she was also absolutely certain that she did not want the boys to lose their father. If she helped Peter and the woman, would they leave her family alone? Right now, that was all that mattered.

Now the bathroom door opens and she waits for him to touch her on the shoulder, to tell her what's been going on, to make some kind of tearful confession and ask for her help. But he gets into bed, sighs, and is soon snoring peacefully. He sleeps when she can't.

And to her it's clear: he hasn't given them the confession they want and she has no idea what happens now.

# TWENTY-NINE

## LEO

Sunday Morning

Leo stays in bed a little longer.

After he met with Serena, he'd driven off, parked three streets away in a dead-end street with little light and waited. His heart raced as he watched the time tick towards his midnight meeting with Peter Denton.

He had picked a place in the park far away from the playground, far away from the streetlights as well. Even with the windows open in the cold air, Leo was sweating.

At 11.55 p.m. he drove back to the park, his eyes darting left and right as he searched for evidence of Serena.

And then he waited and waited.

The man never came. At 12.20 p.m., Leo knew it was over.

He never came to the meeting because he was full of shit. Leo had allowed himself a congratulatory laugh in the car on the way home. Peter Denton was all bluster and this whole thing would go away now. He couldn't believe he'd let the man get inside his head, and he vowed again to not let his life get side-tracked by a woman again. He needed to concentrate, to build up his career, to settle into his suburban life with gratitude.

He had fallen for a very sophisticated scam. They had obviously done their research on him and read about the accident. Leo remembers his name appearing in a few news articles at the time, mentioning him as Peter Elias's boss and that he was a witness for the prosecution. He'd been a good witness, letting everyone know about Peter's drinking and about how awkward and strange the kid was.

The man who killed that kid is in jail, where he belongs. Serena's dedication to the scam was to be admired and Leo thought it would be a good idea to apply that to his next few sales. Researching clients before he pitched them, doing a deep dive on Instagram and Facebook and maybe even court records would give him an edge of sorts. Maybe even an edge over the great Jason Black.

The letters in the locked drawer of his desk gnawed at him. He should never have kept them but he looked at them as a kind of insurance policy against any future issues with Peter Elias. One day the man would be out of prison and if he tried to contact Leo, to come at him for any reason, the letters would serve as an example of continued harassment for years. Leo never wanted to read them, why should he? The right man was in jail and that's where Peter Elias belonged.

*Maybe you should have read them.*

He brushed away the thought.

'Peter is where he belongs,' Leo repeated to himself as he pulled his car into the garage. He had a strong sense that by next week his whole life would be back on track and he had made the decision to stay on the straight and narrow. He would agree to counselling with Diana. They had been completely in love once. They could be again. He was certainly going to steer clear of strange women for a while. When he had got into bed, after a warm shower, he'd felt relaxed with the knowledge that he had escaped unscathed from his whole terrible month. Only his car had actually suffered and that was almost funny. Cars could be repaired.

He hears the boys running downstairs to get breakfast. They're in a hurry to get to the park for their hour of soccer without supervision. It was genius of Diana to offer them the time alone at the park on a Sunday morning. They never said they didn't want to go and he got a peaceful Sunday morning.

He stretches luxuriously, looking forward to the day ahead. He might even take the family out for lunch. Everything is looking so much better this morning as the winter sunshine creeps in around the curtains. So much better.

# THIRTY

## MELANIE

She's had a sleepless night, knowing things will escalate. She turns over in bed as her phone trills.

'Hello,' she says without looking at the number. Of course it will be him.

'I'm in control of this now.'

'Please, just give me more time. I can contact him again. I can tell him what's at stake.'

'No,' he says. 'No, I'm done being kind. Meet me at the house. This ends today.' He hangs up.

She sits up and puts her head in her hands. This has gone too far.

She cannot help the tears that fall. This is not who she is, not who she ever meant to be. Revenge is never the answer. Too many people get hurt, including those who seek revenge. Perhaps they are the most hurt of all.

Peter turns over in the bed and looks at her, his blue eyes filled with concern.

'What do you think he's going to do?' he asks Melanie.

Melanie shakes her head. Last night she had told Peter to stay home, to stay away and let her deal with Leo. She hadn't wanted him to watch her speak to Leo, hadn't wanted to risk his anger spilling over right there in the park. Instead, she had taken someone else along, someone whose desire for revenge was deeper and darker than hers, than Peter's. Someone who is infinitely more dangerous than Leo Palmer can fathom.

'I think he's going to finish what we started,' says Melanie. 'I think he's going to destroy Leo Palmer.'

# THIRTY-ONE

## DIANA

Sunday Morning 11 a.m.

*If you want Sawyer to come home, your husband needs to tell the truth.*

*If you want Sawyer to come home, your husband needs to tell the truth.*

*If you want Sawyer to come home, your husband needs to tell the truth.*

The words from the text circle in her head; not just a text, but a threat, a threat against the life of one of her children. Who are these people? Who has Peter Elias become that he could do this? And why did she ever agree to get involved? She should have gone straight to the police, then to Leo. All the reasons she had for going along with this scheme come back to her but it made sense when only Leo was involved. She never imagined they would involve her children.

In the kitchen, she rinses a breakfast plate again and again, the warm water running over her hands.

She should never have allowed the boys to go to the park this morning. She should never have allowed them out alone. They are all that matter and now one of them is in danger. She got involved in this... scheme? Plot? She has no idea what to call it but she only got involved to protect her children, to protect their safe, comfortable lives.

Rowan comes to stand next to her. 'That plate is clean, Mum,' he says gently, turning off the tap and placing it in the dishwasher.

'Oh, sorry, darling, I...' She can't find any words.

'Mum, why aren't we looking for Sawyer? On television they call the police when someone is lost. I don't understand,' he says.

Diana looks at her son, at the child who seems to breeze through life without giving anything a second thought. He has his brother's face and right now he has the same worried posture of slightly hunched shoulders that Sawyer always has.

'Dad's going to sort it out,' she tells him and he nods, wrapping his arms around her waist and holding on tightly, something he hasn't done for at least a year. In his ten-year-old mind, Dad can sort out everything.

'I'm scared,' Rowan says.

'Me too, baby,' she says. 'Me too.'

Once she had shown him the message, Leo's phone buzzed as well and as he read the screen, he bit down on his lip hard, drawing blood. Bastards,' he muttered.

'We need to call the police,' she said. 'We need to call them right now. You know who has him, Leo. I know you do.'

'No, no police, see?' He showed her the message he had received.

*No police or Sawyer doesn't come home. Come to the Denton house.*

'The Denton house?' she asked him. 'Where is that?'

'It belonged to an old lady, the reluctant seller. I told you about her.'

'You know who has him, Leo, and you know why they've taken him,' she said.

Leo stood up. 'No, I don't. I have some idea but I need to... I will find him and bring him home.'

'You need to admit it, Leo,' she said, her voice rising, 'this is—'

'Just be quiet,' Leo yelled, waving his hands at her. 'Just shut up and let me think.' He moved around his office, picking up his stapler and putting it down again, lifting a glass paperweight and holding it in his hands.

'No, Leo, you know what this is...' she began, determined to bring it all out into the open but he held up his hands, raised his voice.

'I said just let me bloody think.' He pushed past her out of his office and went into the kitchen where he grabbed his keys.

Diana followed him. 'Leo, I know what's happening...' she tried.

'No, not now,' he yelled. 'I will bring him home, I promise.'

'We need to call the police now,' she demanded.

'No,' screeched Leo. 'They won't hurt him. This is about me. I'll go and get him now. I know where he is.'

'I'm coming with you and I'm calling the police. I know—'

'Diana,' said Leo, grabbing her by the shoulders and shaking her a little, 'stop talking and let me go, just let me go. I'll be back soon.'

'No, Leo, we need to get the police...' she said, standing her ground, but he pushed past her and ran to the garage, and in a moment, he was gone.

Diana stood in the kitchen, stunned. Her hands automatically reaching for the dirty plates on the kitchen table.

Now she pulls her son tighter to her, regretting everything she has done in the last few weeks. How could she have been stupid enough to get involved with these people?

Is Peter Elias capable of hurting her son?

The young man had sent them a gift basket when the twins were born, two blue teddies and two little blue singlets. 'I bet his mother told him what to do,' Diana had thought and then she had written him a card, thanking him. He wouldn't hurt a child.

It's been five minutes since Leo left. If she calls the police, would Peter and the woman actually hurt Sawyer?

It's not a chance she can take. Surely, they don't really mean Sawyer harm. They want justice. They want Leo to face his own lies.

'I should have waited for him,' says Rowan in a small voice and she looks down at him. 'I'm older and I should have waited.' The two minutes older that Rowan has on his brother is the subject of many arguments with Rowan frequently calling his brother, 'the baby' but now her child is ashen faced and desperate; he has failed in his role as 'the big brother'.

'Oh baby, no,' says Diana, holding him by the shoulders and looking into the green eyes he shares with his father, 'this is not your fault, not at all. It's just...'

'Why haven't we called the police?' Rowan asks again.

Diana tries to imagine explaining this. How will she get the words out; how will she tell them the whole story? Is it enough to just tell them he's missing and how long will it take for them to ask their questions? Does Sawyer have that kind of time? And what will she tell them about what she knows? About how involved she is?

It doesn't matter. She has no choice. She pulls out her phone and begins dialling triple zero. She'll say he's missing and tell them he's at the Denton house. They will know how to find it. They will bring her son home and end this whole ugly scenario.

As she's about to press her call icon, a text message on her phone sends a surge of relief through her body because she thinks it will be Leo telling her he has their son. But as she opens it, she knows it's been too short a time.

*You need to come here.* Diana peers at the number. It's from the woman. She deleted the picture of her breasts but it's definitely from her. There is an address.

'Rowan,' she says, struggling to keep calm, 'you need to go next door to Mrs Stephanson and stay with her.'

'What? No,' yells Rowan.

'Rowan, go, now,' she commands. 'Tell her that I had an emergency.' She knows the older woman is home because she can hear her lawnmower going.

'Why can't I stay with you?' he protests.

'You just can't, now go.' If she gives in just a little bit, Rowan will convince her to take him with her and she can't have that.

There's no time for a discussion and no time to call the police. She needs to go now.

'Okay,' says Rowan, throwing up his hands and walking towards the back door that leads out of the kitchen.

'And Rowan,' she says, 'don't tell her anything, do you understand?'

Rowan doesn't reply, just slams the kitchen door on his way out.

Diana rushes to get shoes and her bag.

In her car she imagines her quivering insides turning hard, turning into stone. She channels the Diana who will end this hideous game even as she curses her own stupidity for not seeing this as a possibility. She will get her son back.

She's not going to let anyone but Leo pay for his crimes.

# THIRTY-TWO

## LEO

He is a raging fire one minute and a terrified child the next.

He arrives at the house, his car screeching to a stop as he yanks on the handbrake. This place was going to make him some much-needed money, was going to help ease his burdens, but instead has nearly cost him his job. He would burn it to the ground if he could.

How had Serena even gained access to this place? He had mentioned the trouble he was having briefly, even told her the address because he was, he has to admit now, boasting about the sale. He wanted her to know he was dealing with multimillion-dollar properties. *Ego-driven idiot.*

Who are these people and how does he save his son from them?

He could call the police right now, direct them here and end this but what then? There would be an investigation and everything would come out. He can't risk that. He can't risk his life blowing up just as he's decided to turn it around, to become a better human being.

Without trying to formulate a plan, he jumps out of the car.

His heart is pounding and there is a pain down his arm as he races up the steps to the front door and smacks his fist against the timber. 'Open up, open up,' he shouts. His mouth is dry and he feels dizzy. What has he done? Why is Sawyer being held here?

The door swings open to an empty entranceway. The slightly musty odour reminds Leo of his first visit here.

'Come in, Leo,' he hears Serena say.

Steeling himself for a physical confrontation, Leo walks through to the living room. *I will kill you both.* His heart misses a beat at the thought of seeing her again after last night. She had still been, even as a scam artist, beautiful, desirable. But now he wants to rip the hair from her pretty head. How dare she take his son.

He reminds himself to stay in control, to stay calm. *You got yourself into this, Leo; how will you get yourself out of it?*

There is a woman standing in the living room, young, with her brown hair in a ponytail. She looks familiar.

'Sit down, Leo,' she says, gesturing to the sofa. Her voice is Serena's voice. But this is not the Serena he knows. He knows her and yet he doesn't.

'Sit down,' she says again and he drops to the sofa.

'Serena?' he asks.

'No,' she says, 'not really.'

It is Serena but she looks very different, even her eyes are a different colour. Serena has blue eyes and this woman's eyes are brown. Maybe he's mistaken? Her hair is tied back and it's the wrong colour. Where has the silky black hair gone? *How could I not have noticed a wig?*

She's wearing jeans and a stretched-out hoodie, a faded logo he can't identify in orange and blue on the front.

'Where's my son?' he asks.

'Safe,' she says. 'But... Leo, you need to tell me the truth about that night. You have to.'

'I want to see my son,' he says. Maybe they don't have Sawyer? But then where is he?

'You'll see him when you tell me about the night of the car accident,' says the woman.

'Why do you care?' he asks her. 'What on earth does it have to do with you?'

'Matthew was my brother,' she says. 'The young man you killed was my brother, Matthew,' she repeats as though he hasn't heard her.

The name comes back to him in a flash. Melanie.

How could he not have recognised her? When he had to testify in court, he kept his focus on the lawyers, never met the eyes of anyone on the jury or those sitting in the audience. But of course, he had looked at them once or twice, at the young woman sitting next to her mother. And he can see that this woman is her, older but her. This is the sister of the man who was killed in the car accident.

Inside Leo there is a collision of worlds, of spaces he has created.

'I don't understand,' he says. *What? What? What? What the hell is going on?*

Melanie sits down in the cracked leather chair Leo himself had sat in as he spoke to Mrs Denton about selling her house.

'I'm going to tell you a story, Leo,' she says.

'I want to see my son,' he demands, his fists clenching. Is it only her here? Is Sawyer here and where is the psycho boyfriend? He could easily overpower her. He could really hurt her. His body starts to rise.

'Don't even think about moving,' she says softly. 'I'm not here alone, but you know that.'

Leo slumps back onto the sofa and nods his head.

'Okay, so let me start at the beginning... over a decade ago, you met a nineteen-year-old man in a store that sold vacuum cleaners, do you remember that?'

Leo nods. He does remember and the churning in his stomach makes him bite down on his lip. How can this be about that? How are Serena and Peter connected? He should have read the letters the man sent him from prison but he knew what they were going to say and he didn't want to read the words.

'Anyway, a younger Leo, who had a pregnant wife at the time, goes into a vacuum cleaner store and meets a man, a boy really, who is a great salesman. You went in with a budget in mind but he talked you up to something more expensive. As you were leaving the store, you turned back and said, "I just spent a hundred dollars more than I was going to." Do you remember saying that, Leo?'

'Yes,' says Leo, his head pounding, sweat forming under his armpits. The pain is back down his arm. *Heart attack? Panic attack?*

'And you gave him your card and offered him a job. Do you remember the man's name?'

'Peter Elias,' whispers Leo.

'Peter Elias, that's correct. Peter contacted you and you gave him a job and he was pretty good at the work, wasn't he?'

Leo can feel the heat of anger running through his body. 'He was fine,' he says curtly. 'You're not getting what you want from me. Where is my son?' he yells.

Leo doesn't even register Serena move but she is out of her chair and standing over him in a second, her hand swinging. He feels the sting of the slap on his cheek and he starts to move.

'No,' she says, pointing at him. 'Sit down and listen. You don't get to talk. You don't get to make demands. Not now.'

Leo drops his head. *I will kill you when I have my son. Once I have Sawyer, you will die.*

'Peter worked for you for a bit and you got along okay and when you had a nice big sale and invited him out for dinner, he went. He let you buy the drinks and the two of you celebrated the sale and got really, really drunk. But then it was time to go home and Peter had driven to the bar, hadn't he? Because he often drove you around, didn't he?'

'Yes,' says Leo.

Serena nods and Leo wonders if he could just leap up and strangle her and then he hears a cough from another room. Could he take on both of them?

'Look...' says Leo.

'Let me finish,' says Melanie. 'Peter didn't want to drive back but you didn't want to spring for a cab and you wanted to get back to the office so you laughed when he said he didn't want to drive and said... and here, Leo, I'm quoting because what you said made quite an impression so the actual words have never been forgotten. You said, "I've driven drunker than this, you big baby, get in the car, I'll drive."'

'That's a lie.'

Melanie shakes her head. 'Please just tell the truth,' she whispers, her eyes shining with unshed tears.

'Just give me my son and I'll go home and this will never have happened,' he says, dropping his tone. Maybe he can reason with her. 'I don't know what Peter has told you – it's Peter who's your boyfriend, isn't it?' he asks, as pieces click into place.

*When did he get out of prison? How long has he been out and watching Leo and his family? You should have read the letters. You got yourself into this, Leo. How will you get yourself out of it? How will you get your son out of it?*

'You need to know he's lying. He lied about everything. It's all a lie,' he says and he can see by the way she's looking at him that he might actually have a shot at her believing him.

'No,' he hears from behind him, 'no, Leo, it's not a lie.'

Leo jumps up from the sofa and presses his back against the window as a man enters the room. A large man with a shaved head.

'Relax,' says the man.

'Who are you?' Leo asks.

# THIRTY-THREE

## MELANIE

Something like pain flits across Peter's face. Leo still can't see him, even though he must know it's him.

'You know me,' says Peter.

'I don't,' says Leo.

'Think hard, Leo, look closely,' says Peter, walking right up to him, standing next to him and looking down. 'Club sandwich and a latte. Can I get you anything else, sir?' he hisses.

'Did you...' Leo gulps, 'did you serve me lunch at a café?'

Peter steps back and does a slow clap. 'Well done, Leo.'

Leo stares at him, a blank look on his face, but then he rubs a hand over his eyes and Melanie can see him realise who he's looking at. 'Peter?' asks Leo.

'Prison really messes with your looks, Leo. Now, before you deny it again, I'm going to finish the story.' He looks at Melanie and she gestures for him to speak. He knows how much this hurts her, to hear these terrible details laid out in simple language. 'Leo was driving and I was in the passenger seat next to him and we came to an intersection and I remember looking up at the light and seeing it was orange and so I said, "Leo, it's orange," and you just said... you just said, "Screw you, orange light," and went through. It was really late and it seemed like we were the only car on the road but we weren't.'

Melanie jumps in, not wanting anyone else to say her brother's name. 'Matty was coming back from meeting his girlfriend for dinner,' she says. 'They'd only just gotten serious and he really liked her. He told me before he went out that he wasn't going to drink because he wanted to be able to drive her home like a gentleman. That's what he told me.' A sob catches in her throat and she sees Peter moving towards her but she shakes her head. She just wants this finished and done.

She remembers the pain of getting the tattoo, the M wrapped in tendrils, remembers the welcome sting of the needle because it gave her something else to think about for just a short time. She never imagined her grief would lead her to this.

And then she thinks about the text she sent as Peter started talking. *Please hurry, please hurry, Diana.*

Peter takes up the story. 'I remember the screaming crash of metal hitting metal and the smell of burning rubber in the air,' he says, still standing close to Leo. 'And then I remember just sitting there for a second and then I looked at you and you were looking at me. "Shit," you said.

'"What happened?" I asked you because I was confused and in shock. You said you would check it out. Remember that, Leo?'

'No,' says Leo. 'You're lying, you're making this up.'

'I sat in the passenger seat waiting and trying to stop myself from throwing up because I knew what was going to happen. I wasn't driving but I was drunk and I shouldn't have gotten in the car with you. I shouldn't have let you drive my car. But I did get in. And I have paid for that, haven't I, Leo?'

'You're lying,' whispers Leo and Peter lifts his hand and wraps it around Leo's throat. Leo's body freezes. Melanie can see his fear, can see his fear for his son.

'Stop saying that,' he hisses. 'Stop talking and let me finish my story.'

Leo nods his head.

Peter moves his hand and throws a look at Melanie, offers her a sad smile. 'I'm sorry you have to hear this again,' he says to her and then he looks at Leo. 'You came back to the car and said, "I think he's dead." Your face was pale, and your nose running and you looked like you were about to be sick as well.

'In the distance we heard sirens and even though they were probably heading to something else, we both panicked. And then you said, "You need to check him, check that he's gone."

'"But you said…" I started to say and you just screamed at me. "You need to check him now!"'

Leo shakes his head but he doesn't speak.

'So that's what I did, I got out of the car and went over to check and that's when I saw Matty, Matthew, who was gone. I saw his head on the steering wheel and he looked like he was just sleeping, like he'd pulled over to take a nap. But his eyes were open. I remember his eyes; how blue they were.'

'Like my dad's eyes,' says Melanie and she can't help her tears and she hates herself for them. She wanted to be strong to get this done.

'I couldn't look at his open eyes so I leaned into the car and closed them, which meant my DNA was on his face. And I told him I was sorry.

'When I turned around, you were gone,' says Peter. 'It was my car. I was standing at the site of the accident. I was drunk. I had touched Matty and there was no one there but me. And then a trucker pulled up to a stop in the intersection and the guy got out. He was on an overnight run and he tried to help but as soon as I started trying to explain, he called the ambulance and then he called the police. I remember him saying, "This kid is beyond drunk," as he looked at me. He had no idea who I was

but, in that moment, I felt like he hated me, like absolutely
hated me. And I didn't blame him. I hated myself.'

Peter walks back and forth across the living room, touching
small objects like the collection of porcelain clowns on a
console.

'I should never have gotten into that car. If I hadn't, if I had
told you that I was going to walk, you probably would have
walked with me. I could have just walked away and I didn't. I
didn't so it was my fault.'

'No, not your fault, not your fault at all because you weren't
driving,' says Melanie.

'No,' says Leo, his voice just a whisper.

'The police investigated my claims. But there was no
CCTV on that particular traffic light yet. And none that they
could find showing us together in the car.

'Leo's DNA was in my car but I usually drove him around if
he was running late for appointments and he'd even driven my
car a few times before so that proved nothing and Leo kept
insisting that he had walked, that he had told me not to drive,
that I was the one who thought nothing of getting into a car
plastered. My lawyer advised me to accept my fate. He told me
that the more I protested, the more I tried to blame someone
else, the worse it would get. No one saw us after we left the bar
and headed to my car in the parking lot. No one could confirm
that both Leo and I got into the car and that, in fact, he got in on
the driver's side. No one believed me and here I am.'

'He's lying,' says Leo.

'You're lying,' hisses Peter, 'still lying.'

'And you're well known for being a liar, aren't you, Leo?'
comes another voice.

# THIRTY-FOUR

## LEO

Leo turns, shock sending another ripple of pain down his arm. There's someone else? How can there be anyone else?

Another man walks into the room. Leo blinks twice and then he rubs his eyes.

His mouth gapes open and closed and finally he says, 'Robbie. Jesus, Robbie.

'Robbie,' he repeats as the man stares at him, his face neutral of expression.

'What are you... I don't...' Leo cannot formulate a sentence.

And then Robbie lifts his arm and Leo can see he's holding a small gun.

'Matthew didn't just have a sister,' says Melanie. 'He had a brother as well. A family. We were a family, Leo, and you destroyed us.'

Leo shakes his head as he understands that everything he has concealed from not just the world but from himself as well is being tossed into the light. In the last nine and a half years since it happened and then through the investigation and the trial, he managed to push it so far down, managed to dismiss it so strongly that he has come to believe that it really happened

the way he said it did. It had been about survival. He was a
father with a young family and he needed it to happen the way
he said it did. Even on the night it happened, he had heard his
father in his head. *Why would you have done something so
stupid?* And he had been determined to not have done the
stupid thing. He made up his mind. He wasn't stupid and he
had not done the stupid thing.

'Where is my son?' he asks.

'Upstairs,' says Robbie, and Leo opens his mouth to call him
but Robbie lifts the gun, points it right at him.

'If you get to see him again, don't blame Sawyer for getting
into the car with me, Leo. He knows me, he likes me. I work for
you. Just like Peter did.'

Leo swallows, his throat dry, remembering a Saturday two
weeks ago when Diana brought the boys into the office on the
way to a soccer game. Robbie had come over to say hello and he
and the boys were almost instantly involved in a discussion
about the next World Cup with Robbie telling them how he
played soccer in high school.

He is surrounded by liars and fakes. He should just tell
these people what they want to hear and get Sawyer and go
home. He'll go straight to the police when it's done. All of them
will pay for what they've done.

Melanie pulls out her phone and Leo can see she is
recording whatever is said. Peter does the same thing. He needs
to save Sawyer but he has a life to go back to after this. Would
telling them what they want to hear destroy all that?

'The worst thing is that we thought we got some form of
justice when Peter got sent to prison for his death,' says Robbie.
'I was overseas, in the army, helping rebuild a village after a
cyclone, and I couldn't be here. My mother and sister suffered
through that trial without me, without my father, but I took
some comfort in the fact that the right man had gone to prison.'

Leo remembers reading an article about the case, vaguely

remembers reference to another brother. 'Listen, Robbie,' he says, 'I think you need to listen to my side of the story. I don't know why you... why you believe him when the police and the jury didn't. I need to tell you that Peter was a strange kid,' he says, ignoring the man staring down at him and concentrating on Robbie who lowers the gun a little, just a little. 'I offered him a job but once I hired him, I realised that he didn't really have what it takes, to be honest. But I felt sorry for him. Most kids grow out of being awkward by the time they're nineteen but he was still all over the place. He could barely do a coffee run without spilling something. I remember taking him to meet clients and having to apologise when he said something stupid. He was sloppy and he was difficult to work with but I felt sorry for him because I offered him the job.'

'That's crap,' says Peter.

'It's okay, Peter,' says Robbie, 'let him finish.'

Peter grunts but doesn't say anything else.

'I was worried about him because he was so young. We have alcohol in the office to celebrate big sales. Martin likes to open a bottle of champagne but it doesn't often get finished. We all have homes to go to. But once Peter started working for us, it was always finished.' Leo speaks quickly, the words tripping over themselves.

'That's just—' begins Peter and then Robbie throws him a look and he's silent again.

'And then, a couple of times, I actually caught him drinking during the day. He would come back from lunch plastered, maybe because he knew he was screwing up.' Leo feels himself warming up to his story as it unfurls into the air. What he's saying feels like the truth. He can even see young Peter Elias weaving through the office after returning from lunch, can see himself pulling the young man aside and telling him, 'You can't be doing this, mate.' The image is clear in his head.

'I can't believe you haven't killed him yet, lying sack of shit,' growls Peter.

'Peter, don't,' says Melanie. And Peter leaves the room, walks away in a huff, and Leo wants to celebrate because now is his chance.

He can feel he's getting to them, feel them believing him. They will release his son and this will be over soon.

'I did have dinner with him that night. I was actually going to fire him but decided against it. I was worried about how much he'd had to drink but I actually thought he was just getting into his car to sleep it off. I walked back to the office, had a sleep and then went home. And then the next morning, I heard what had happened and then I got a visit from the police who told me that Peter was blaming me. I was shocked, really shocked, because I had been trying to help him get his life back on track,' says Leo, shaking his head. 'I went willingly into the station to make a statement because I knew what the truth was. I explained everything to them and they believed me; they're the professionals and they believed what I was saying. They knew he was lying. You've both been taken in by a criminal. He's lying about everything.'

Finally, he runs out of words but he needs to repeat himself so he makes really sure.

'So, you see, he lied. I wasn't there. I walked back to the office. It was just him and he was trying to shift the blame. I don't know why he thought it would work.'

This is not a scam, not something designed to simply take ten thousand dollars off him. This is about revenge. But he can get out of it.

All he needs to do is have them shift their focus back on to Peter and it will be over. Has he done enough? They are quiet, digesting what he's said, another little nudge and he'll be there.

'Do you really think the police and the prosecutor and everyone else involved in the case is so stupid that they would convict the wrong guy? They questioned me. For hours we went round and around and then they released me because they knew I was telling the truth and Peter was lying.'

'You should just kill him now,' says Peter who has come back into the room. And Robbie lifts the gun higher, aiming.

'I agree,' he says.

'Wait, wait,' yells Leo. 'What do you want? Just tell me what you want.'

'A confession,' says Peter, and Melanie and Robbie nod.

'You planned this, all of you planned this?' asks Leo.

'When I worked for you, I was Peter Elias because I was using my mother's maiden name. My father was such a complete dropkick that by doing that I felt like I was distancing myself from him a bit. But my mother wasn't much better so now that I'm out of prison, I have decided to go back to my father's surname. Because it's my grandmother's surname as well and out of everyone who raised me, she is the only one who has truly loved me no matter what. Want to know what it is?' He looks down at Leo who suddenly understands. He thought they were in the Denton house because Serena-Melanie had broken in and then, maybe because Robbie had a copy of the key, but that's not why.

'Denton,' he says softly.

'That's right,' says Peter. 'You approaching her was a lucky coincidence or unlucky for you. We were just starting to figure out what to do and there you were Leo – trying to charm an old woman into selling her home. And you didn't even wonder why she changed her mind so quickly. All you could think about was the money you were going to make. All you could think about was yourself but that's always been your only concern and now you, Leo Palmer, are going to pay for what you've done.'

'Why bother?' asks Leo. 'Why bother with any of it? Why not go to the police?'

'I went to the police, remember?' says Peter. 'I told them

what really happened but you denied it. You just denied it and let me get sent to prison. What kind of a man does that?'

'What are you three hoping to achieve here?' asks Leo, knowing that his only hope is to keep these psychopaths talking.

'We want a confession,' says Melanie.

'But that's just it, S— Melanie, you don't actually want the truth, you want the lie. You want to hear the lie that you've been taken in by.'

Peter leaps towards him, roaring, 'Liar, liar,' grabbing him by the shirt and shaking him as Leo hears his teeth click-clack together. He may just kill him; this giant monster man may just kill him... and then there is a pounding on the door.

'Leo, are you in there? Sawyer, Leo... open the door.'

# THIRTY-FIVE

## MELANIE

Peter looks at her and she can read his fear. This wasn't supposed to happen. None of this was supposed to happen. She knew, deep down, that Robbie wouldn't stop. But maybe if Diana is here, he will give this up.

There is a pounding on the door again. 'What do we do?' asks Peter.

'Diana, run,' shouts Leo and Peter punches him, not hard, but hard enough to shut him up. Leo's body is jolted back and his head hits the window with a thump. He touches his mouth, where there is a spot of blood, and shakes his head.

'I'll go,' says Robbie and he leaves the room.

Everyone freezes while Robbie opens the door and then Diana appears in the room.

'Well, look at that,' says Robbie. 'The whole family's here,' and he smiles. 'Minus Sawyer's brother, of course, but that's okay, Melanie and I are also minus a brother.'

The woman with long brown hair tied back into a high ponytail looks around the room. She locks eyes with Melanie.

'My name is Diana Palmer,' she says, 'and I assume you are the woman he's sleeping with.'

'Oh God,' says Leo, hanging his head.

'What on earth is going on here?' says Diana. 'Where is my son? Where is Sawyer?'

Robbie lifts the gun and points it at her. 'Sawyer is safe upstairs.'

'I want to see him,' says Diana.

'I want you,' says Robbie, extending his arm holding the gun, 'to sit down and shut up.'

*How do I stop this? How on earth do I stop this now?*

She and Peter should never have involved Robbie. She hadn't understood how long Robbie's anger had simmered, how large his despair over his brother's death had grown.

Robbie had always been their protector. After their father died, it was Robbie who organised things, helping their mother to stay on track with the funeral, making sure she and Matthew were okay, sorting out the estate. He was only twenty-three but he had aged overnight, become a man.

And then Matthew died and Robbie stepped up again, only two years later. A week after Matthew's funeral she had looked at him and noticed silver hairs threaded through his usual dark brown. She had not known that he was a man who had returned to his job in the army carrying the burden of guilt because he had not been able to protect his little brother.

'Leo,' says Robbie, his gun still trained on Diana, 'we want a confession or we will kill you.' His voice is soft, his tone gentle. Melanie cannot locate the real Robbie in the words.

He could be offering Leo a drink, just mentioning the weather, anything but telling a man he is going to kill him.

When Matthew died, Robbie was in the army, helping restore flood-ravaged villages overseas. He had returned for the funeral, held them together as they grieved, but was not there for the trial, instead going back overseas to do his humanitarian work. Melanie had resented his desire to go back to his job as she supported their mother through the trial. She had wondered at his ability to squash his grief down and get on with his life. But he had not been getting on with anything. He had been existing parallel to twenty-five-year-old Robbie, just like Melanie had been doing with her nineteen-year-old self. And that Robbie was filled with rage. When Melanie told him that she was speaking to Peter, he was furious, his anger so huge and so dark that Melanie understood that her older brother's grief had never really been dealt with.

'He should rot in there,' Robbie yelled when she told him what Peter wanted.

'I agree,' she replied, 'or at least I did agree but now that I've started speaking to him, I feel like I have to listen. He's served eight years.'

And when Peter was released from jail and Melanie met with him, she shared his story with Robbie who had been sceptical, disbelieving.

'I think this guy is lying,' Robbie told her.

'What does he have to gain?' Melanie asked him. 'He's already been to prison so what does he have to gain now?'

She introduced Peter to Robbie. And after listening to Peter talk, Robbie was also convinced by his story. And Robbie would also not accept that there was 'nothing they could do,' about Leo's lies.

Ideas had emerged slowly over many days and when Robbie left one job to take another in a larger firm, he took a two-month break in between so that they could put their plan into action.

'Sit down, Leo,' says Robbie. 'Sit next to your wife on the sofa.'

Leo doesn't move from his position at the window and then Robbie waves the gun in his direction and he sits down, taking Diana's hand, an act that seems unconscious.

Leo stares up at Robbie. 'I don't think you will kill me, Robbie,' he says. 'In fact, I think you are going to let me and my family go.'

'Leo, please,' says Diana. She moves her hand from his.

Melanie is amazed. The punch has not changed anything. His wife being here has not changed anything. Leo is revving up again and Melanie can see that he still believes he can just get out of this.

Leo leans back on the sofa, relaxed, confident. 'I like this little set-up the three of you have got and it's clever; I mean, I never suspected a thing but what I don't know is why you went through with the last few weeks. I didn't need to sleep with Serena, I mean Melanie, and I didn't need my car damaged, my office trashed. I didn't need any of it. Why not just drag me in here and demand I confess?'

Peter sighs. 'Let me ask you something, Leo: why do you think we did it?'

'I think you're cowards, all three of you,' Leo taunts. 'If you were going to kill me you would just have done it. And now we're here and your last hope is some sort of forced confession that I will never agree to; and even if I do say anything, I will immediately deny it and say I was coerced. You're holding my son hostage, for God's sake. You need to let us go,' he says, moving his hands up and down, calming the flames of this terrible fire of a situation. 'If you just let us go, I'll pretend this never happened. I'm sure I won't see you again, Robbie, and that's fine. The accident was a long time ago. I'm a different person now.' It's so obviously a lie.

'If you are a different man, why did you sleep with me?' Melanie asks.

Leo shrugs and offers her a sickly smile. 'I mean... a beautiful woman comes on to you at a conference... who could resist?'

'Oh, Leo,' moans Diana. 'Please, Robbie,' she says, 'I understand your anger, I do, but you need to let Sawyer go. This is not how you get what you want.'

Robbie shakes his head. 'And if you've changed, Leo, why did you push an old lady into selling her house?'

'It was good of my grandmother to help, wasn't it?' says Peter to Leo.

'I couldn't believe it when she told me who had been sniffing around her house. When I told her what we wanted to do, she agreed to put the house up for sale with you and try to back out, just to see, just to check that you were still as awful a human being as you were back then,' says Peter, 'and you forced her to go ahead with the sale. We watched you do that, Leo. We were here, listening to every conversation you had with her, listening to every awful, badgering lie you told her. We were here, in another room, listening to you threaten an old woman.'

There is a moment of silence. Melanie sees a flicker of fear across Leo's face. He had not realised he was being listened to.

'What?' he asks, dumbfounded.

'Yeah. We were here. Do you want to hear some of what you said?' Peter asks.

Leo shakes his head but Peter has already pulled out his phone and hit play, turning the volume up. Leo's voice fills the room. 'And the thing about backing out of a sale is that no one will ever trust you to work with them again. I mean, the real estate market in Sydney is small and I'll let everyone know—'

'Stop,' says Leo, 'just stop. You had no right to do that. It was a private conversation.' Peter stops the recording with a small smile.

'One I'm sure Martin would be interested to hear,' says Robbie.

'You think that will lose me my job?' spits Leo. 'She wanted to sell. I may have pushed a little but we all do. It's the nature of the game. But you want to send that to Martin, fine. He'll support me.'

'The house didn't sell, Leo. I spoke to the Campbells and told them a mistake had been made and that they were not to speak to you about it. It didn't sell,' says Robbie. 'I explained it to them. I told them she was old and confused and now her grandson was getting a lawyer involved. They were happy to have their money returned for the deposit.'

'This is ridiculous,' says Diana. 'You need to let us go now.'

Robbie holds up the gun and releases the safety catch. He aims it directly at Leo's head. 'I was the best marksman in my year,' he says. 'I trained as a sniper but I preferred to do the humanitarian work. I'm pretty good with a handgun as well.'

'Robbie,' warns Melanie.

The one thing she had wanted to do, what she and Peter and Robbie wanted to do, was to make sure Leo was still the same man.

Melanie knew she needed to put her body and her soul on the line, despite both Peter and Robbie telling her not to do it. Peter particularly hated it, telling her again and again to stop, to just leave it to him and Robbie.

She wanted to make sure, very sure, that the man they were going to hurt, the man whose life they set out to destroy, was still that kind of man, still a man who would have a car accident that resulted in someone's death and then just run away and let another man take the blame – because maybe, just maybe, he wasn't. It was possible that Leo had used the eight years while Peter was in prison to reform his life, to change who he was as he grappled with the guilt of letting someone else take the terrible blame for what he did. That's what Melanie had almost hoped to see, almost hoped to be able to report to Peter and Robbie.

But something that she will never tell either of them is that she wanted Leo to experience some level of torment. There was a chance that they would never get what they wanted and if that was the case, she needed him to suffer, even if it was only for a little bit. It's not something she is proud of but it's something she can admit to herself.

Robbie had also been looking for evidence that Leo was now a better man. Using Peter's grandmother to see if Leo would do the honourable thing had been an easy idea; tempting Leo into an affair had not been. Finding out he was a serial cheater had simply confirmed what Melanie suspected the day she met him. Leo has not changed at all. He has not been mired in guilt and shame. Instead, he has simply dismissed the accident and Peter from his mind and got on with being the same man he always has been.

But still she hoped that if she got close enough to him, if he trusted her enough, he would tell them what they needed to hear. And no one else would be involved. She has failed spectacularly. And now they are on the brink of something terrible and she doesn't even recognise her own brother.

'You need to tell them the truth, Leo,' says Diana. 'Tell them the truth so they let us go home.'

'I'm not—' begins Leo. And Robbie takes aim.

'Stop,' screams Diana. 'I only agreed to help you because you promised no one would get hurt.'

'What?' says Leo. 'What?'

# THIRTY-SIX

## DIANA

'You helped them,' spits Leo. 'You helped them?'

The look her husband gives her is filled with betrayal and loathing, fifteen years of love, of building a life, of sharing children, wiped out in a second.

Diana shakes her head. 'I had no choice, no choice, Leo. They were going to destroy you and they still will. Just tell them what they want to know. I've read the letters, all the letters he sent you. I know the truth, you know the truth, just tell them. Our son is upstairs, Leo, how can it even be a question?'

'You...' says Leo, running his hands through his hair.

'Tell us, Leo,' says Robbie, 'or maybe I shoot her.' He moves the gun to Diana's head and she feels her heart leap into her throat.

'Why are you letting this happen? Why did you agree to taking Sawyer, how could you?' she says to Melanie.

'I...' She shrugs her shoulders, shakes her head and Diana understands that this has gotten out of control.

Robbie is in control of this now. And he has no compassion for Leo, for Sawyer, for her.

He is an angry brother, a man with a score to settle.

'Please, Leo,' she says, 'just give them what they want.'

'Tell us the truth,' says Robbie. 'Tell us, Leo, tell us.' He moves the gun from Diana's head to Leo's head and back again.

'Speak, Leo,' he spits, 'tell us,' he raises his voice, 'tell us, tell us,' he yells, 'tell us.' He is screaming now and waving the gun and Diana knows that he may kill one of them without meaning to. His face is a deep angry red and his movements jerky. 'You took him from us and then lied. We had already lost so much. Tell us or I swear your son at home will lose a brother like I lost a brother.'

'No,' gasps Diana, her body sagging. She leans forward and puts her hands on her knees to hold her body up.

Robbie starts to move towards the stairs, towards Sawyer.

'Tell them, Leo, for God's sake, tell them,' screams Diana and Leo raises his hands.

'Okay,' he yells, 'okay, okay.'

And finally, Leo, her husband, the man she thought she knew, begins to speak.

# THIRTY-SEVEN

## LEO

'It was my fault,' Leo whispers. 'Are you happy?' He looks at Robbie. 'It was my fault.'

'Tell us everything, Leo,' says Melanie, menace in her voice.

Leo is exhausted. He looks at his wife and then he drops his head into his hands. She has betrayed him, worked with people who hate him to destroy him. Why? Why would she do this to him? How has this happened? How has their marriage turned into this? *Why do you think it happened, Leo? What have you done to make her do this?* He hears his father's voice, hears the voice of the man who never let him get away with anything.

He understands he has driven this kind, empathetic nurse who takes care of mothers and their babies, and loves her sons with everything she has, to this. He has done it.

'I'm so sorry,' he cries. His whole wasted life confronts him, every stupid decision he's made, every terrible thing he has done, all the people he has cheated and the women he has slept with when he had someone at home who loved him. He has never cared enough about the things that matter and he is sickened by himself. He has no idea if he and Diana are going to make it out of here but he needs her to survive for the boys. If he confesses, if he tells the truth, then they will let her and Sawyer go. *Please God, make them let my family go.*

'I was driving the car that killed Matthew,' says Leo. 'I was drunk and I was driving and I asked Peter to get out of the car to check on him and then I... I ran away.' He hangs his head as he speaks, not wishing to look at anyone, the shame of that moment coming back to him.

He had pushed Peter into driving because he didn't want to wait for a cab. He already knew that Diana was going to be angry about him being out. Work was one thing, getting drunk with your junior was another. The boys were only six months old and still not sleeping through the night. And he hated being home. Diana was exhausted and the kids were a nightmare and it was easier to just be out, at work or with Peter, drinking and watching all the pretty young things in the pub.

He had grabbed the keys when Peter refused to drive, taken them from the young man's hand and gone over to his car, even as he felt his body sway a little. He'd had way too much to drink.

'Leo, please, I'll pay for the cab,' he remembers Peter saying, something that angered him. It wasn't a question of money. He knew that if he came home in a cab, then Diana would know he'd been out drinking and he was hoping to hide that from her, hoping that he could sneak in and have a quick shower in the downstairs bathroom. His car not being at home in the morning was a giveaway. He needed to get back to the office car park where he had left his car. It was a short drive, such a short drive. Nine years ago, the pub across the road hadn't opened yet but the one he and Peter had been at was so close. But Leo didn't want to walk back. Why didn't he want to walk back? He was drunk and drunk people make terrible decisions.

Peter had reluctantly got into the car beside him and Leo had adjusted the seat. His legs were shorter than Peter's legs.

He had gripped the steering wheel, concentrating hard, his senses heightened as his brain filled with cottonwool. He was aware of the street lights, of the few cars on the road, of the trees outside bending in the wind and of Peter, holding his door handle, gripping it.

He doesn't know what happened then, how he missed the light at the intersection go from green to orange but he does remember saying, "Screw you, orange light." He does remember the terrible shock of registering that he was going to hit the small sedan going through on the green light. He does remember jamming his foot on the brake and it being too little, too late. He remembers time slowing down and then suddenly speeding up.

The kid looked dead. He did and Leo saw what would happen, even through the haze of alcohol, he knew what would happen.

And his woozy brain kicked into gear. When Peter got out of the car, he adjusted the seat back to where Peter had it, his own clarity amazing him. And then he wiped the steering wheel with his tie.

And then he just got out and ran. He was fit and strong, the wind freezing, and he ran all the way back to the office, almost proud of how quickly he got there.

And then – and here, even as he thinks about this, he cannot believe he actually did it – he got into his car and drove home. He showered downstairs and got into bed next to his sleeping wife, relief warm in his alcohol-riddled veins as he fell asleep.

'Tell us everything,' says Melanie and she puts her mobile phone on the coffee table.

Leo starts speaking and he doesn't stop until he has finished. He lays bare the whole sordid story. Diana shifts on the sofa as he speaks, her body moving, leaning in the opposite direction to his. Leo speaks with his gaze on his wife who recoils slightly more with each dreadful new detail.

'I was worried about you and the kids,' he says finally to Diana. 'I knew I would lose my job and probably go to prison.'

'But you let Peter go to prison,' says Diana. She shakes her head, wipes away a tear. She stands. 'If you have what you wanted, I would like to take my son home.'

'Why do you stay with him?' asks Melanie, incredulously, and Leo realises he is listening for her answer. Will she still stay with him after all this?

'I won't, not anymore,' she says, and Leo feels the pain down his arm again, the clenching of his heart. He's lost everything.

Robbie nods his head. 'We're going, you stay and we're going. And we will be taking this recording to the police.'

'Fine,' says Diana.

Leo cannot look at them, any of them.

He can't go to jail. There's no way this will actually work. The recording will be inadmissible in court. They must know that. He just needs to see his son. Everything else can be sorted out if Sawyer is okay.

'My son,' he whispers.

Melanie hands him some small keys. 'He's upstairs,' she says and Leo would like to rip her head off. But he darts upstairs and unlocks a bedroom door sealed with a padlock.

'Sawyer, Sawyer,' he calls frantically, opening the door and seeing his son on the bed, still for a moment. The pain shoots down his arm but then Sawyer turns over and jumps off the bed. Leo's relief on seeing him move slices into his body.

How could he have wanted more than this? Sawyer barrels into him and his arms close around him tightly.

'I'm sorry, Dad, I'm sorry,' he whimpers.

'No, no, no, it's not your fault, not your fault,' rasps Leo.

And then Diana is there and they are all hugging and crying.

'Stay here,' says Diana, 'wait for me.'

Leo wants to protest but he cannot speak. He nods, holding onto his child, holding on to his life.

# THIRTY-EIGHT

## MELANIE

She waits outside the house. 'Just go, I'll be there in a minute,' she tells Robbie and Peter and they do. Everyone is hungry and tired but Melanie knows she needs to wait.

She pulls her jacket around her as the August wind whips around the streets, tossing dry brown leaves in the air.

Finally, Diana comes out of the house, pulling the front door closed behind her. She is only wearing a jumper and she wraps her arms around herself as she comes towards Melanie.

'How could you have let that happen?' hisses Diana as she gets closer to her. 'How could you have involved a child?'

Melanie holds up her hands. 'I didn't know what he would do until I got to the house. I had no idea he would bring Sawyer, I promise you, but he... Robbie is so... he needs help. I know he needs help.'

'You should have stopped him, told him to take my son home. I can't believe this happened.'

'I couldn't,' says Melanie, 'don't you understand? Robbie was in control. I tried to prevent this; everything I did was to prevent this.'

'How can you love a man like that? How can you love a

brother who would do such a thing?' says Diana, wiping tears from her face.

'I would never have let him hurt Sawyer, never, never,' says Melanie. 'But Diana, how can you still want to protect Leo? I'm not the first woman he's cheated with. Why are you still with him?'

Diana sniffs, wraps her arms around herself and then her shoulders sag, the fury leaving her body. Melanie knows the conversation could go around and around forever. Love is complicated. 'I can't have him in jail,' says Diana. 'Can you understand that?'

'I can, yes.'

'Is it done now?' asks Diana. 'Are you done? Did you get what you wanted?'

Melanie shrugs her shoulders. 'It doesn't bring Matthew back, does it?'

'No,' says Diana.

Melanie looks across the street at the houses opposite where lives are being lived like any other street and where no one knows what happened here today.

'You need to stick to the bargain, Diana – or he goes to prison,' she says. It's not that simple and Melanie knows that Diana is aware of this. The recording would probably not be admissible in court. She and Peter and Robbie would certainly face charges for what they have done but Melanie is betting on Diana keeping her side of the bargain. There are other ways to ruin a life and Peter is willing to use everything at his disposal to ruin Leo's life if he feels the man is getting away with it again. Not every injustice is set right in a court of law. Some are set right in the court of public opinion.

Diana nods. 'I will tell him everything I discussed with Peter. I'll let him know that you have the recording and you're prepared to use it. I'll stick to the bargain. I want him to be there for the boys. I don't want them to grow up with a father in prison. You have the choice to take the recording to the police but I promise, I will do exactly what I told you I would.'

'Okay.' Melanie nods.

'Okay,' says Diana and she turns to go back to the house. But then she stops and turns back. 'I'm so sorry about your brother. I don't think I ever said that but I am, deeply sorry.'

'Thank you,' says Melanie, her eyes filling with tears. She turns away before Diana can see them and goes to find her brother and Peter.

The plan had been clear. Destroy Leo Palmer's life. His life as a husband and father and his life as a real estate agent. Leave him with nothing and no one.

That was the plan.

And it started with Robbie joining his agency and befriending him as he collected information on the man.

And now it's over and none of them will ever be the same. Robbie needs some help, that much is obvious. Maybe they all do.

Where do you put terrible grief? What do you do with it and how do you keep living?

Robbie's anger is frightening. Can he let go now? Can any of them?

Melanie rubs her arms, the cold creeping in under her clothes, and then she starts to run. Their cars are parked around the corner. She runs, the cold air hitting her face and drying her tears. She runs towards something or away from something.

# THIRTY-NINE

## LEO

He and Sawyer are sitting on the sofa, waiting for Diana. He is holding Sawyer's hand and the feel of it is so strange; he wonders how long it has been since he has held one of his sons' hands.

How will he ever explain what has happened here today? How will he get both boys to keep all this a secret? Can he even ask that of them? They have been through so much.

Diana comes back into the house.

'They're gone,' she says, her face pale.

'I need to go to the police. I need to tell them I was kidnapped. We need to go now.' Some small part of him still clings to the desperate hope that he can turn all this around, that he can reclaim his life.

'No, Leo,' she says sadly, shaking her head. 'Sawyer, go and wait outside,' she commands and he looks like he's going to protest but meekly gets up and leaves.

Diana sits down in front of him.

'We're not going to the police. Because if we do, then I will tell them that your confession is the truth. I have given Melanie copies of all the letters from your desk drawer. They tell their own story as well. You were driving the car that killed that young man and you let someone else take the blame. I don't understand what kind of a human being does that.'

'What are you saying?' asks Leo, grateful that his son is not hearing this.

'I'm saying that I've convinced Melanie not to go to the police. But they have some conditions... some things that I have promised will happen.'

Leo sits back, shock making him numb but anger coming quickly. 'Screw them. I don't care. How can you not back me up? You're my wife. Do you want Rowan and Sawyer to grow up with a father in prison? Is that what you want? Because it will change who they are forever. They need to be reported.' He's so tired he could sleep for a week. And now he's angry as well. One betrayal on top of another. When does it end?

'No, Leo. We won't be doing that. We won't go to the police and if we don't, they won't. And then no one – especially you, Leo – goes to jail. The boys never have to know what you did or why this happened.'

She pauses, letting the truth lie between them. He is stuck. He cannot tip the scales one way without them tipping back.

'You killed someone,' she says. 'You lie in your work and you cheat people and you've cheated on me. You're not... not a good person, Leo, and you need to find a way to be better.' His wife doesn't look at him as she says this, instead focusing on her hands, fiddling with her wedding ring, twisting it around and around.

Only when she is done speaking does she lift her head and gaze at him with tear-filled eyes. He can see the pain he's caused but he doesn't let that stop the fury rising inside him.

'Then leave me,' he spits, standing up. 'I'm going to the police and getting all of them arrested.'

'You will go to jail, Leo. You will lose everything,' says Diana firmly. 'I will make that happen; I promise you.' She folds her arms. Her voice is strong even with her tears still drying on her cheeks.

'Yeah, we'll see about that,' he sneers. 'They have a forced confession and no real evidence. It's my word against theirs and if it comes to that – against yours as well.'

Diana juts out her chin. 'You're right Leo. It may not end with you in jail but I want you to imagine what it will cost you to have this investigated. They have the letters and the recording. I will speak against you rather than for you. And you should know this. Peter is prepared to launch a civil case, to actually sue you in court for his time in prison. You can say what you like in a civil case. He will go to the press. He will smear your name in whatever way he can. You will lose everything, Leo, including me and you will see your children on weekends, if you're lucky. It will take years and your sons will find out everything you did on the internet, probably at the same time as their classmates find out. People can get cancelled for a single post on social media. Imagine what happens when Peter starts telling his story to the whole world.'

Leo sees it all right in front of him as though it's actually happening, sees his name everywhere and the way the boys start to look at him, sees cameras in his face as he pushes into court because the media love stories like this. Would he survive that? Would his career survive it? And if he has no career and no Diana and the boys look at him with disdain or worse, disgust – what does he have left? Who even is he? His shoulders slump with the weight of it all. He has lost this battle and this war. He can feel it. But he tries one more time to get his wife to see sense.

'What am I supposed to do here, Diana? You know those other women meant nothing. Serena or Melanie, whatever the hell her name is, meant nothing. It's all just for fun and I'll stop, I promise I'll stop.'

'You will,' agrees Diana, 'because here's what's going to happen.'

Leo sits down again, the fog getting thicker, despair weighing down his body as he listens to his wife speak and he finds out exactly what is going to happen to his life now.

He has a momentary pang of guilt for Peter because when he was put into jail, he tried to tell everyone the truth but no matter what he said, no one believed him and there was nothing he could do.

In court, when Leo was there to testify, he had avoided looking at Peter, knowing what he was doing to the young man's life. But he couldn't help but catch a peripheral glimpse of him, couldn't miss the shaking of his head as he silently refuted everything Leo was saying.

When he was on the stand, Peter only answered 'yes' or 'no' to questions, barely speaking unless he had to, but Leo could feel everything he wanted to say in the air. During the investigation and the trial, Leo had slept with his phone in his hand, sure that at any moment the police would call and tell him they knew he had lied. But they had no proof and Peter could not convince them. And because that was how it played out, Leo managed and has, for nearly a decade, managed to convince himself that this is what was meant to happen. Peter went to prison because there was nothing he could do to save himself.

And Leo understands that now, right now, with the recorded confession and his wife willing to act for other people. There is nothing he can do to save himself either.

Leo listens as Diana explains all of it, horror descending on him as he realises that he may not be going to prison but that he is actually *going to prison*.

# EPILOGUE

## Leo

Leo ladles some thick vegetable soup into the bowl of the man standing in front of him and he tries not to wrinkle his nose at the smell coming off him. His shabby grey coat is voluminous on his skinny frame and his tufted grey beard hangs to his chest.

'Thanks, mate,' says the man. He shuffles along in the line, grabbing four bread rolls, stuffing one hungrily into his mouth.

Glancing at the clock on the wall, Leo sees he has another four hours to go. Time crawls forward minute by minute at the soup kitchen. He's been on his feet for hours already and when it's time for a break, he will get offered the same food he is offering the people in front of him: under-seasoned hearty fare that he hates but eats for something to do.

He is here all day Saturday and Sunday from 9 a.m. to 5 p.m. The other volunteers can't believe he is so willing to give up so much of his time. Leo would bask in their approval but he's too tired to care.

His weekends of open homes and pub lunches are over and will be for another eight years. Eight years.

It's been three months since the Sunday Sawyer was taken by those people.

Leo is no longer in real estate, no longer the owner of a beautiful Porsche, no longer who he was.

Now he drives a small second-hand sedan, not unlike the one Matthew was driving the night he died.

Leo ladles some more soup into another bowl held by an old woman. She grins at him, gaps in her teeth.

He comforts himself with the shower he will have at home, scorching water washing the overcooked vegetable smell and body-odour-air of the soup kitchen away.

When he's done, he will spend the night with the boys, playing board games, something that would be helped with a few drinks but he's not allowed that either. Diana will go out with friends and he can feel that, sometime soon, she will start dating. His wife is a beautiful woman.

They are separated but still living together in the same house.

Prisoners need supervision and his wife is head prison guard.

Leo drinks a lot of coffee now, more than five cups a day, desperate for the jittery sensation it gives him after more than two cups. At least it's a different feeling.

When he lies down at the end of the night, it will be alone in the guest room. No alcohol, no recreation. He's not allowed to date.

He's allowed to go running and he does every morning at 5 a.m., out the door and onto the road, pounding along with country music loud in his ears, his day ahead kept at bay for just a little while. He is leaner now than he has ever been, which is great because he eats a lot of junk food now as well. At least she left him that.

When the twins are eighteen, he will be free to leave. When the twins are eighteen. Peter spent eight years in prison and Leo will pay for every day the young man was locked away.

'Give us a bit more, mate,' says a kid, someone who can't be more than sixteen, who has just taken his place in the queue.

Leo sighs, spooning extra into the bowl, wishing for a moment that he was the kid who, despite his circumstances, has youth and his whole life ahead of him.

Monday to Friday, Leo works in a bank as a teller. The bank is one branch in an area that used to have five branches and it services a mostly elderly population.

The work is boring, monotonous, time slithering by so slowly, some days he's convinced the clock is actually moving backwards. Everyone he sees is already angry because of the queues and the wait times. Leo hates it. He hates all of it. On his worst days he curses Melanie and Robbie and Peter as he runs, damning them all to hell over and again with each step he takes. There are times when he reflects that his punishment is right for him but they are few and far between.

'You'll change as the years go on,' Diana says if he questions why she is allowing Melanie, Robbie and Peter to hold his confession over his head.

'It's destroyed our family, our lives,' he says.

'You had already done that, Leo. Now you're here at night, present and engaging with the boys. This is for the boys.'

Diana has a new job during the week doing night shift at a large hospital. Leo walks in the door and she walks out so the time available to convince her to drop this whole thing is limited. He tried for the first couple of months. He tried to talk to her and text her and email her, just so he got his thoughts straight. He offered to move to another state, to live somewhere else but still take care of them financially. He begged and pleaded but Diana has not budged.

'This was the deal, the bargain I made to keep you out of prison.'

'You should have just let Robbie kill me,' Leo has said, more than once.

Diana just shakes her head at him. 'One day you will realise how much you still have.'

Will he?

Every now and again, he sees Melanie or Robbie or Peter. They pop up when he goes to get lunch at work, when he stops for petrol and even on his run. They're watching him.

There are moments with the boys sometimes when he's grateful for the time, fleeting moments. And there are moments at work when he manages to explain something to an elderly man or woman and they are so grateful he cannot help taking some pleasure at their thanks.

Maybe they will become frequent moments, maybe he will be a better man after all this but he doesn't like to think about that for too long. The years roll out ahead of him, monotonous and boring in a way that he had never imagined possible. He can't believe he was bored with his life before all this. What on earth had he been thinking? He'd had it all. He'd had the perfect life and he'd screwed it all up.

'This is a just and fair punishment,' Diana says whenever he questions her.

'How come you get to decide that?' he has asked her.

'I get to decide it in the same way that you decided that your need to get your car, that your life of freedom, that your needs were more important than the life of a young man, than the freedom of another and the hurt feelings of your wife. You've done all the deciding up to now, Leo. Other people are in charge and will be until the eight years are up.'

Is his punishment just and fair? On his morning runs, he sometimes fantasises about just leaving, about taking some cash and getting in a car or catching a plane and disappearing. They wouldn't look for him, he thinks. And that thought is not as comforting as it is meant to be. Because maybe Melanie, Peter and Robbie wouldn't look for him but maybe – neither would Diana and the boys. They would dismiss him from their lives and no one would care where he was or what had happened to him. So he stays because maybe, he can do his time and still have a life after that where he has his children and one day, grandchildren, in his life. But that doesn't mean he is any less reluctant to be living this way. He hates it and he's sure he will hate it until the last day of his sentence.

'Careful, don't spill it,' says a woman in front of him and Leo rights his ladle and fills her bowl.

He glances at the clock on the wall again.

Three hours and fifty minutes to go.

Seven years, eight months, fifteen days, three hours and fifty minutes to go.


Diana

She checks the time on her phone. Leo will be home soon, weary from his day at the soup kitchen, disgruntled and sad.

If she looks at him for too long or spends a little too much time with him, Diana can feel herself bending, breaking.

How terrible would it be to just stop all this?

It would mean she wouldn't have to be his jailer. She would be free of the man who cheated on her, broke her heart. But then who would make sure that he was doing the right thing? She made a promise and she is trapped here for the sake of her sons, just as Leo is.

On bad days, when all she wants is her freedom, she reminds herself of the desperation in Peter's letters, of just how much Melanie and Robbie lost and of how much she nearly lost.

She is not entirely convinced that Robbie wouldn't have hurt Sawyer. She had only met him once before that terrible Sunday but he had seemed so genial, so kind. But if he could kidnap a child, what else could he do? She worries about that, about her complicity in keeping quiet about what happened. But they are all keeping quiet, all complicit.

The nightmares about what happened haunted her for weeks until she found her new job. It is, somehow, easier to sleep during the day.

She finds she loves the busyness of the large hospital and being able to use her midwife skills again.

Watching babies come into the world, seeing the joy on every parent's face when they have the delight of a safe birth and a healthy mother and baby is a balm for her soul.

The boys are still confused about what happened that Sunday.

'Robbie was angry with Dad,' is what she and Leo settled on. But they have explained that the boys don't need to worry because they will never have to see Robbie again.

'But why?' asked Rowan.

'Because I fired him,' Leo said shortly. 'And I promise he has gone very, very far away and he will never see you again.' Diana had allowed that to stand.

She knows that the boys are sceptical, that they still have questions. But right now, her instincts tell her it's too much for them to process. She will tell them the truth but she's hoping it can wait until they are a bit older.

She questions the decisions she made to get involved, even though she had no idea they would resort to kidnapping a child.

Is this the better outcome? Sawyer who was taken and Rowan who was terrified for his brother are traumatised by what happened but Leo is still here to raise them. Is this the better option for her boys? She has no real idea. But they are here now and it's done and the best she can do for her sons is move forward.

She chose a normal family life, as normal as it can be under the circumstances.

'I didn't know what to do when Robbie took me to the house, Mum,' Sawyer told her. 'I thought it was to watch a soccer game and that Rowan would be there. I was scared and when they locked me in the room, the windows wouldn't open and I didn't shout because the lady told me to keep very quiet. I was scared and I didn't know what to do.'

'It wasn't your job to know what to do, sweetheart,' she replied. 'This was an adult problem you got mixed up in, but it's all over now.'

What else can she say?

Both boys now have mobile phones – something Diana never wanted for them until they were much older. Sawyer doesn't make a move without consulting her and the walks to the park are on hold for the next few months.

Their sense of safety has been shattered and if Diana thinks about that for too long, her anger at Robbie, at Melanie, at Peter screams through her body. But then she asks herself, *when does it stop?*

They did what they did because they were hurt. They lashed out and now if she lashes out and goes to the police, what will happen then? What will happen to Leo? When does it stop?

Now, she has decided.

Leo being home so much is a wonderful gift for the boys. Will the time he is spending with them help heal the wound of the trauma they both experienced? Diana is hopeful that what happened will eventually become an indistinct memory for both of them.

She will never forget it but she tries, each day, to put it in a box in her mind so that it doesn't torment her.

Tonight, she is going on a date with a doctor from the hospital named Julian. His wife died five years ago. He's an obstetrician and over the last month of working together, they have formed a close friendship. Tonight, they are having dinner for the first time. 'I have no idea how to do this,' Julian said when he asked her out.

'Neither do I,' she told him. He knows she's separated but she has not explained her strange living situation and she has no idea how she will do that. Perhaps that is a problem for another day. It's likely that this will just be a friendship because she's not ready for more than that just yet. The boys are her priority and always will be.


In the weeks following that Sunday, the boys didn't argue at all. Instead, they stayed close, following each other around the house, sitting together and choosing to play different computer games so there was no competition. Rowan's status as the big brother has been firmly entrenched in his mind. Now Diana worries he may be too protective of Sawyer. Robbie was the big brother in his family as well and perhaps those are the children who grow up with the heavy weight of responsibility on their shoulders whether they want it or not. Wrapped up in Robbie's extreme anger, Diana could see his guilt.

'Mum, Mum,' says Sawyer, bursting into her bedroom.

'I've told you to knock,' says Diana.

'Oh, sorry, sorry,' he says, going back out again. He knocks extravagantly on the door.

'Come in,' she calls and he opens the door again. 'Rowan wants to have pizza. It's my turn to choose and I don't really want pizza. I want Thai food.'

Diana smiles.

They are slowly making their way back to where they were. She can see that there is something unbreakable between them so she sees Sawyer asserting himself as a good thing.

'Then Thai food it will be,' she says.

'Where are you going?'

'Out to a movie with a nurse from the hospital,' she lies

easily. She will meet Julian at the restaurant. She turns in the mirror, trying to see herself as Julian might. Her hair is longer now and she's wearing it down and the new dress in pale pink suits her complexion.

'Okay,' says Sawyer, darting out of the room and then she hears him calling, 'Dad, Dad, I want Thai food; don't you want Thai food?'

'Whose turn is it to choose?' asks Leo. And the twins talk over each other.

In the kitchen, Leo is having a cup of coffee and eating his way through a packet of caramel chocolate biscuits. She hates having this much junk food in the house but Leo needs it.

'You look nice,' he says quietly when he sees her.

'Thank you,' she says and holds his gaze for just a moment before she looks away. She cannot let herself feel sorry for Leo. He never felt sorry for anyone.

'I won't be late,' she says and he nods, picks up another biscuit.

'I'll be here,' he says.

'I know you will.' She nods and then before she leaves, without thinking, she gives his shoulder a squeeze and as she makes her way to her car she hopes and prays that this will get easier for him, easier for both of them.

It can never be easier for the family who lost a child so she has to be strong, remain firm.

She made a promise and she intends to keep it.

In the car she takes deep breaths, admonishing herself not to be silly because she knows Julian. But she feels herself on the precipice of something, something new and different, and she feels in control of that as well. For a long time, her life has been dominated by the needs of others but now, with Leo home so much, she has space and time for herself.

Divorce will happen one day when the boys are older and Leo has served his sentence but until then, this will have to do.

Parking the car, she thinks of Leo and the boys, imagines them playing board games and laughing, wishes her estranged husband an easy evening. Love doesn't just disappear. Grief doesn't just go away. But Diana hopes that Melanie and Robbie and Peter are finding a way forward as well. That's the best she can hope for. It's the best all of them can hope for.


Melanie

It's a Monday morning and Melanie stands on the pavement, staring through the large glass window of the bank, watching Leo try to explain something to an old woman who is shouting at him in a language he doesn't understand. Her grandson stands next to her, translating, but every now and again the boy rolls his eyes as if he can't believe that Leo is such an idiot.

She does this occasionally, finds him, watches him. He doesn't know that he is being tracked by her and Robbie and Peter. Diana has a tracking app on her phone and it automatically shares Leo's movements with them. That was part of the deal.

Over the past few months, Melanie has been waiting for Diana to renege, to go back on her promise and force Melanie to make a decision about turning Leo into the police. Melanie doesn't know what she will do then and she is grateful that Peter and Robbie are in this with her.

Leo's shoulders drop as the young boy lectures and he nods his head. Even from where she is standing, Melanie can see a deep flush covering his face. Good. He deserves humiliation. He deserves boredom and humiliation and years ahead where his freedom is curtailed.

Is he paying the price for what he did?

Maybe. But what price would be enough? Nothing will bring her brother back. Nothing will return Peter's eight lost years. From his wife's perspective, he will never not have cheated on her, never not have found other women to share his bed with.

On the occasions she does watch him, he never seems particularly happy. He has lost the gleam in his eye, the spring in his step. Is it enough?

She knows he is being denied sex and alcohol, that he has lost the career he loved, that he spends his weekends helping others. Is it enough?

Leo nods and nods and then he types on his little computer at his counter and finally the old woman and her grandson seem happy.

The queue for a bank teller stretches out the door, most of the people waiting are old, many are complaining in an obvious way. Leo's day will be long and tedious and then he will go home to care for his sons while his wife – from whom he is separated – goes to work. It's not fair on Diana but it's what the woman wanted for her children. A father at home is better than a father in prison and Melanie hopes she doesn't eventually resent the sacrifice she is making. But then what would her mother have sacrificed for Matthew to be alive and safe? What have she and Robbie sacrificed to make sure the right person pays for the crime of his death?

Melanie sometimes feels like she is watching the family on television, watching Leo's despair and Diana's commitment to the plan they all agreed on.

She rubs her face. It will have to be enough.

Robbie has rejoined the army. 'I need to do something good with my time,' he told her but she worries for him. He is still so angry. Hopefully some time helping out in distressed communities all over the world will give him some perspective. He and Peter speak a lot, conversations that she never hears but Peter says they discuss overwhelming anger and what to do with it.

They have every right to their fury – all of them do. But how long do you let it control you? Peter seems to have found a way to push it aside and Melanie just hopes that he can help Robbie do the same.

'Ready,' asks Peter. He is not as interested in watching Leo as she is. Every day he is out of jail is a gift for Peter. His pastries are bringing more people into the café and Joe is allowing him to do more and more of the day-to-day running. He's an older man, looking forward to retirement.

'He said he would be happy to leave me in charge for a few days a week,' Peter told her last week. 'And maybe in a few years, he may be willing to sell to me.'

Peter is doing something he loves and he's good at it. All he wants to do is put his days in prison behind him. He has his confession and the people who matter to him know the truth.

He could turn Leo in, sue the police, be paid compensation for his time in prison, but he does not want to do that. 'How much more of my life will that take? How many years of dealing with the police and lawyers and time in court, and for what? Money? I'd rather make the money with my hands, build something good, live a good life.' Melanie cannot fault his logic.

But it's harder for her. She still has to tell her mother that she will take Matty his lunch or that Matty is visiting her next week. And every time she does it, another crack appears in her soul. She still needs Leo to pay.

'Mel, babe, you ready to go?' Peter asks.

'Ready,' she says, smiling up at him. She takes his hand and they turn, leaving Leo to his queue of people.

They have both taken the day off and are on their way to visit his grandmother in her new apartment on the ground floor of a nursing home where there are medical staff on call at all times.

The house that was never sold, has now been sold to a developer for a lot more than Peter expected. After buying an apartment for his grandmother, he has put the rest aside for the future that he can see coming.

Melanie enjoys her visits with Judy, Peter's grandmother, loves talking about what Peter was like as a child, but mostly she loves seeing grandmother and grandson together. Peter is twenty-nine and heavily muscled and he keeps his head shaved but sometimes when his grandmother strokes his cheek, Melanie can see a five-year-old boy and she lets herself imagine what their children will look like.

They walk along the road in the warm spring air, a light breeze carrying the scent of jasmine.

'Is it enough?' asks Peter, as he does each time she drags him with her to check on Leo.

She shrugs. 'No, yes, I don't know.'

After they have shared lunch with Judy, they will go over to her mother's care facility and spend some time there. Melanie will introduce Peter to her mother and tell her that they are getting married, just like she did last time and the time before that.

And then they will stay a while until her mother asks her to take Matty his lunch.

And Melanie will nod and smile, even as her heart cracks, and tell her that she will. She will close her eyes briefly and see Matty standing next to the canteen, a smile on his face.

And it will have to be enough.

# A LETTER FROM NICOLE

Hello,

Thanks for reading *His Double Life*. If you enjoyed this novel and want to keep up to date with all my latest releases, just sign up at the following link. Your email address will never be shared and you can unsubscribe at any time.

*www.bookouture.com/nicole-trope*

This is one of those novels that changed a lot along the way. Diana only emerged later in the edits and now when I read her chapters, it feels like the character had to get strong enough to appear.

I know not all readers will agree with the decisions she made but hopefully you will understand them.

Melanie Serena was a fascinating character to write. She is such a lovely woman but her brother's death affected her terribly and knowing that the wrong person went to prison was more than she could bear.

Leo is not a nice man. But I feel like he is being adequately punished and if he can be there for his sons, that is, perhaps, one good thing he can do in the world.

I see Peter and Melanie having a wonderful future together, despite the strange way they connected in the beginning. I wish Peter well, knowing that he is not the first or the last person who will be let down by the justice system in his country.

If you enjoyed the novel, I will be so grateful if you leave a review.

I love hearing from my readers – you can get in touch through social media or Goodreads. I try to reply to each message I receive.

Thanks again for reading,

Nicole x

facebook.com/NicoleTrope

x.com/nicoletrope

instagram.com/nicoletropeauthor

# ACKNOWLEDGEMENTS

Thank you to Ellen Gleeson for a brilliant and thorough edit. The book is so much better for your insightful changes and I'm so grateful to be working with you.

I would also like to thank Jess Readett who never says 'no' to any request and is always on board for anything I want to do.

Thanks to Donna Hillyer for the copy edit, and to Liz Hatherell for the always meticulous proofread.

Thanks to the whole team at Bookouture, including Jenny Geras, Peta Nightingale, Richard King, Alba Proko, Ruth Tross, Mandy Kullar and everyone else involved in producing my audio books, selling rights and getting my novels out into the world.

Thanks to my mother, Hilary, who reads every novel.

Thanks also to David, Mikhayla, Isabella, and Jacob and Jax.

And once again thank you to those who read, review and blog about my work and contact me on social media to let me know you loved the book. I love hearing your stories and reasons why you have connected with a novel.

Every review and message is appreciated and I do read them all.

## PUBLISHING TEAM

**Turning a manuscript into a book requires the efforts of many people. The publishing team at Bookouture would like to acknowledge everyone who contributed to this publication.**

### Audio
Alba Proko
Sinead O'Connor
Melissa Tran

### Commercial
Lauren Morrissette
Jil Thielen
Imogen Allport

### Cover design
Sarah Horgan

### Data and analysis
Mark Alder
Mohamed Bussuri

### Editorial
Ellen Gleeson
Nadia Michael

**Copyeditor**
Donna Hillyer

**Proofreader**
Liz Hatherell

**Marketing**
Alex Crow
Melanie Price
Occy Carr
Cíara Rosney

**Operations and distribution**
Marina Valles
Stephanie Straub

**Production**
Hannah Snetsinger
Mandy Kullar
Jen Shannon

**Publicity**
Kim Nash
Noelle Holten
Myrto Kalavrezou
Jess Readett
Sarah Hardy

**Rights and contracts**
Peta Nightingale
Richard King
Saidah Graham

Made in the USA
Las Vegas, NV
28 April 2024